Spawn

DRAGONS OF THE CROSSROADS BOOK 4

LORI SALTIS

VAGABOND TALES

Copyright © 2023 by Lori Saltis
ISBN: 9781967542048

Cover art by DAZED Designs

Published by Vagabond Tales.
All Rights Are Reserved.

My heartfelt thanks to everyone who encouraged me on the journey to write this series.

Tony's blowing up my phone, which means he knows what happened. No message, of course. He doesn't do messages because he expects me to call him back. Instead, I stare at the wristwatch he gave me for my birthday. Unlike me, it's shatter-proof. I feel like I've broken into a million pieces.

Penny and I have been in London for a day, and we managed to turn the world upside-down. We've become moving targets, not just for our enemies, but also our families.

I glance around my sort-of prison. I'm in an old train carriage with wood-paneled walls, gold-curtained windows, and plush, red velvet benches. The door isn't locked and there aren't any bars, but I can't leave. Getting past the guards isn't an issue, but I'd get lost in the labyrinth of the London Beggar Abode. They took over an abandoned subway station and everything that went with it, including the decommissioned trains left behind on the tracks. And since they're the Beggar Clan, they repurposed those trains into living quarters, and even have a private rail line that crosses the city. Pretty damn impressive, but you gotta be resourceful when you don't have a dragon backing you up.

A train rumbles through a nearby tunnel, making the car rattle, a constant sound throughout the Abode. I guess they're used to it. I guess I gotta get used to it if I'm stuck here. There's a bathroom, a mini-fridge, and even Internet access on my phone. Am I a prisoner or merely awaiting the pleasure of Mad Maud, the Beggar Chief, who has even more reason to hate me now?

My phone buzzes again. After a long sigh, I open it, but don't answer. Instead, I tap the SpyNot app and scan the carriage. It alerts me to a tiny video camera lodged in an upper corner, almost hidden by the curtains. I stand on a bench, look in the lens and say, "Really?" before yanking it loose and tossing it outside. The guards loitering on the platform stare at me. I wave. They don't wave back. Story of my life. Nobody likes me.

I close the door, settle on the bench, tap the Missed Call screen, and ponder Tony's name. I don't call him that. We're Chinese and I've always called him Big Brother, even before we knew we were brothers. Secrets, lies, and murder conspired to turn us into enemies. Thing is, we love each other. When I was a kid, I thought he was the greatest person on Earth. Part of me still does. My thumb hovers over his name before tapping the screen. My stomach clenches and I hope he doesn't answer.

But he does, with a tense "What have you done?"

I roll my eyes. No matter what I do, he's always going to make me feel like I did it wrong. "I healed Matthew. I mean, we healed him. Penny and me."

"Have you seen the news? There was a terrorist attack in London, right next to his hospital. Was that you?"

"No. I mean, yeah. I mean, yeah, but we weren't the attackers. We were attacked, and it wasn't terrorists. It was Uncle George."

"Tell me what happened."

So, I tell him about healing Matthew, almost being murdered by his parents, and being targeted by the sniper, and how Penny and I mingled our *chi* to save our bacon. I don't tell him our father killed Penny's dad. The words stick in my throat and I can't make myself say them, partly because I'm still gutted, and partly because I don't want him hating Dad more than he already does.

I hate Dad more than I can say, but I also love him. It tears me up inside and tossing that Tony's way can wait for our next conversation.

I weenie out with, "So, we're back in the Abode now. We'll probably be here a few days until Mad Maud can arrange for us to leave London."

"You are indebted to the London Beggars." It figures that's his takeaway. I did my best and all he can offer is disapproval.

"That's easy to say when it's not your ass on the line."

He's silent. Probably thinking he wouldn't ask for help regardless of the situation his ass was in.

I huff. How do I make him get it? "It wasn't just me. I had Penny and Matthew to consider. I needed help from our allies. They offered, and I took it."

"Putting us further in their debt."

"You wouldn't do the same if it were May and Aaron?"

He huffs because he hates it when I'm right. "You have the Yin Pearl, which will rally people to our side. You must return immediately. The clan needs your leadership."

Except they don't. I'm a shitty leader. Tony's much better and everyone knows it. What he's really saying is he needs me to give him cred, which isn't true, but there's no telling him that. Discovering your uncle is your father does things to your self-esteem, so I can't blame him.

"I will arrange for you to fly home tonight."

"No." Crap. I can omit things with Tony but lying is impossible. He'll smell it on me, even through the phone. I think quick. "Um, Matthew needs a fake ID so he can travel." See? No need to add that Penny and I need our passports doctored because we entered England illegally, so to speak. "I don't want him and Penny traveling without me, cuz, you know Uncle George…" I trail off as I feel the glow of the Yang Pearl spread across my chest. "Someone's coming. Gotta go. Bye."

I end the call and stare at my phone. What's the chance Tony will accept being Dragon Son after he finds out I hitched a ride to London with Jade Dragon? Zilch.

I pull the Yang Pearl from under my shirt. It's got this glow, more of a sensation than something visual. The Yin Pearl is leading Penny to me, or rather to the Yang Pearl. No wonder the Dragon Son and his wife were such an unbeatable combination back in the day. I sense her entering the platform and I jump up, ready to defend her against the guards. As I slide open the door, I hear her voice, putting the purr in persuasion.

"Of course, I have permission to be here. I'm Mad Maud's niece, yeah? I can go anywhere in the Abode. You can ask her if you like. I'll wait."

Charm. It's a helluva drug. The guards stare at her for a moment, dazed, before waving her on. She strolls away, light-footed, like the dancer she is. My heart skips a beat to the tune of her walk. She approaches the car, sees me, and smiles.

Okay, I was wrong. Someone does like me, against all odds, including murder.

As Penny steps inside, she looks no different from when I last saw her, but somehow she changes everything. The dark, musty cabin becomes warm and bright with the glow of her presence.

She perches on a bench as I slide the door closed. "Hey."

I sit beside her. "Hey."

"Nice carriage."

"I guess."

We lean back, but don't touch. We can't. That sliver of space between us holds too much feeling. She stares at the ceiling for a few moments before sayings, "So, we killed someone."

I look up, too. They really had nice wood paneling back then. "Yeah."

"I feel like I should feel worse about it than I do."

"Well, he was trying to kill us. It was totally self-defense."

Penny tugs on the red silk cord around her neck, pulling a small, polished *Wu Lou* gourd from under her shirt. She examines it for a moment before twisting the center, unscrewing the narrow top from the wider bottom. The Yin Pearl tumbles into her palm, twinkling with multicolor sparks, like an opal, and casting a soft, bluish-white glow on her face, making her look like a fairy princess. "These things are scary powerful. What was the Two Dragon Clan like when they had all three pearls?"

"Scary powerful. Unbeatable. That's why we've been the head of the Crossroads for hundreds of years. The Yang Pearl alone was enough to keep us in place."

"What will you do when you get back the Wisdom Pearl?"

I've already thought about that, so I answer right away. "Drop it in the ocean."

She squints. "What if some shark swallows it and becomes this mega-powerful shark?"

"You mean, like, Sharkzilla?"

"Yeah."

"That'd be so cool."

"I know, right? Let's totally do it."

We exchange grins and then sighs as the light moment passes and darkness returns. Penny scoops the Yin Pearl back into the gourd and draws her knees to her chest. "What happens when we get back to San Francisco? Do we give the pearls to Tony?"

I wish. "No. He won't take them, and even if he did, May

can't use the Yin Pearl while she's pregnant." My chest tightens. I don't want to say what I have to say, so I stall. "Are you thirsty?"

She gives me side-eye. "I guess."

I slide off the bench and open the mini fridge. "Would you like water or," I frown and squint as I hold up a bottle full of purple liquid, "Rib…"

"Ooh, Ribena. I'll take that."

I take one, too, because why not? I have my answer after I twist off the top and take a sip. My mouth twists against the dark, carbonated, wine-y flavor.

Penny grins after a long, blissful drink. "You don't like it?"

"It's different." I like how it turns her tongue purple. That makes me want to have a purple tongue, too. I take another swallow and manage not to shudder. It's not as bad as the first sip.

"Actually, that's good," she says. For a moment, I think she's still talking about Ribena, until she adds, "It'll be easier for us to go against George if we still have the pearls."

The carbonation burns in my throat and chest. I shake my head. "No, Penny. You're done. I take the pearls and go back to San Francisco. You stay here with your family, where you're safe."

She scoots away, twisting so she can face me full on. Her eyes are full of green outrage. Her purple tongue lashes me. "My father died because of these pearls. You think I'm just going to walk away? And do you think your uncle is going to leave my family alone? He made two attempts on my life today. I know how to use the Yin Pearl. That makes me dangerous to him. He wants me dead and I'm not going down without a fight."

"But you've already done so much. I don't want you to die, like your dad did, because of my family."

"My family won't be safe unless I stay in the fight. I'm the only one who can use the Yin Pearl with you. How else can George be defeated?"

She's being upfront, so I need to be, too. "I want you in the fight with me, more than anything. I don't want to do this alone. I just… I don't want you to die."

"We live on the Crossroads. I choose my battles, the same as you."

"I know." It's hard to put into words, so I stutter through my thoughts. "Thing is, I guess, I don't want anyone else involved. I don't want anyone else to die. If I had my way, it'd be me against Uncle George, winner take all. But if he wins, he takes the Yang Pearl and that would be bad for everyone." I throw up my hands. Purple juice sputters out of the bottle. "Damn it." I wipe my hand on my jeans. "I don't know what I'm trying to say."

Outrage drains from Penny's face. She reaches over and squeezes my knee, damp with Ribena. "You want to protect the people you love. I get that. Don't you get we want to protect you, too?"

My throat hurts as I whisper, "But I messed up."

"No, you didn't. You're stuck cleaning up other people's mess. That's two different things. Anyway, I made my choice. I'm not leaving this battle 'til it's over. End of story." She clinks her bottle against mine, leans back, and takes a chug.

Okay, then. To be honest, I'm happy. She's a warrior, the same as me, and fucking powerful. Who am I to stand in her way? I'm glad I don't have to do it alone. The Dragon Son was never meant to be alone. He was always supposed to have a partner with the Yin Pearl. Maybe that's where Dad went wrong. He couldn't handle all the power by himself. From what I'm learning, his father had also left him holding a bag full of secrets and grief.

I take a sip of Ribena and enjoy the flavor. It tastes like victory.

The door slides open. Gareth stands in the doorway, staring at us in that pale, intense way of his, reminding me who I am. The son of the man who murdered Gerry.

Penny

Gerry's spirit has departed, and Gareth is feeling it. That devastating lack of him.

I stand and hold out my hands. His long, sensitive doctor's fingers curl around mine and squeeze. He whispers hoarsely, "I felt him."

Tears fill my eyes. "I know. Me, too."

"I thought I was getting over it, missing him, and then…" His voice trails off as he ducks his head.

I want to reassure him, tell him that Gerry will return next Samhain, but truthfully, I hope not. I hope he's departed this world for the next. It's not good for a spirit to linger too long. It keeps the living from moving on as well. "I know, Pa."

"It wasn't just that. Bridie took you and Kai and disappeared. As if we hadn't all been part of one family."

"Try to forgive her. She was being threatened by the Gerry's family and manipulated by Matthew's parents."

"I know. I just talked to her. She said she did it for Gerry, that he'd want me to be safe." His voice chokes on the last few words.

I look away, taking a deep breath so my eyes don't fill with tears.

Gareth clears his throat. "So, I forgive her. Everyone else, not so much." His gaze hardens as he glances over his shoulder at Lennon. "Helena wants to see you. Both of you."

Lennon nods. Guilt silences him. Guilt that isn't his own. It's unfair, but now isn't the time to challenge Gareth about it.

We follow him into a cage-like lift, the same one I rode down on. Gareth tugs the lever on the gearbox to select our destination. We stand shoulder-to-shoulder as it rattles and squeals its sluggish way up from the depths of the station. Too loud to talk, which is fine by me. Pretty sure Maud's going to give us an earful. The cage shudders to a heart thudding stop. Gareth yanks open the door and steps out, striding ahead without looking back. Yeah, we're in for it.

He leads us through a series of corridors to another abandoned platform storing decommissioned trains, forgotten since the 1960s. The Beggar Clan refurbished them into living quarters, including the guest carriage where my family stayed after Gerry was killed. Matthew and Helena stand outside the door. Both frown at the sight of me and Lennon.

Matthew holds out the phone. "Your mother wants to talk to you."

"Is she still on the line?"

He shakes his head, his eyes moving from me to Lennon as if he's responsible for my misbehavior. "You need to talk to her in private."

"Why? Is something wrong?"

"Just call her."

"Okay." I glance around, because privacy is an issue. "Um, where?"

"You and Matthew will stay here." Helena nods toward the guest carriage. She turns to Lennon. "Dragon Son, you can bunk with the single men unless you find that objectionable."

No special treatment, despite his rank. That is objectionable, but Lennon simply nods and says, "Thank you, Beggar Chief."

I chew my lip, wanting so badly to speak, but knowing it's not my place. Helena might be my aunt by almost-marriage, but she's Mad Maud, head of the London Beggar Clan. I don't have any say in matters between the Beggars and the Two Dragon Clan.

"You have my permission to move between the common room and your quarters." Helena's eyes narrow in at me. "Penny, the same. I forbid the rest of the Abode to you both without escort. Understood?"

"Yes, Beggar Chief," Lennon says without hesitation.

When I'd been here before, I could go wherever I pleased. She's punishing me for my friendship with Lennon. As if that won't make us more determined to be together. I know I'm technically an adult now, but seriously, why are adults so thick?

Helena turns to her brother. "Gareth, take Matthew to get his ID photos taken. Dragon Son, I'll take you to the bachelor quarters. Penny," She nods for me to enter the guest carriage.

Lennon touches my mind. *They're afraid of us.*

He's right. I hadn't thought of that. I'm so used to them all being authority figures, I haven't considered they might find my new powers frightening.

I wish they'd just say so, I reply.

But then they'd have to admit it and they don't want to.

He's right. *Let's just play along. It's only for a few days.*

He mentally nods, and we share a smile as he turns to follow Helena.

As Matthew leaves, he gives me that look, the one I know so well. It's a look he and Gerry shared, one that demanded I join them in protecting Bridie from the worst of the world. I always resented that look. I was a child. Why did they expect me to be stronger than my mother?

Because I am. Because they raised me to be. Just as Bridie's parents raised her to be weak and dependent. She rebelled and legged it with her lovely lads, but some things are engrained and can't be changed. Inside the carriage, I settle cross-legged on the bench and take a deep breath before tapping the phone.

Bridie answers on the first ring. "Darling?"

"It's me, Mum."

"My strapping girl!" She gasps happily before burbling on. "The hero of the hour. You did it. You saved our Matty."

Nice as her praise is, I sigh, because here we go. "Lennon and I both saved Matthew, Mum. And we had a lot of help."

"Lennon. Yes, of course. Is he there?"

"No. I'm by myself."

"Oh, good."

"Why is that good?"

Her voice becomes breathy. "Well, I have a lot to say to you in private. First, the Wongs. I don't have words for how horrid they are or how much harm they've done to our family."

No argument there. Matthew's parents allowed us to believe he was dead for three years. Then, after arranging for me and Lennon to heal Matthew, they betrayed us to steal our pearls. They claimed they did it all for their son, and maybe they believe that, but I know they did it for themselves, to get in good with George Lau.

"Matty told me everything." Bridie clears her throat. Her next words strain out. "He told me Lennon's father killed Gerry."

I close my eyes.

"You must understand that this changes everything. You have to cut ties with Lennon."

"No, I don't."

"Yes, you do. It's for the best."

"Are you going to cut ties with Matthew because his parents tried to kill me?"

"Of course not. It's… it's not the same."

"Yes, it is. What if they'd succeeded? Would you tell Matthew to sod off?"

There's a silence. Then she speaks in a quiet, strained tone. "No, but it would change things between us. How could it not?" She sighs. "Look, you've done your part, yeah? Lennon can take the Yin Pearl back to San Francisco and carry on with his clan's feud. You and Matthew will stay in London with the Beggar Clan, and Kai and I will join you as soon as we can."

And there it is. I'm being forced to choose between Lennon and my family, just like I knew I would be, but it's more than that. What's being dangled before me is my heart's desire to return to London and my old life… no, not my old life. It can never be that, not without Gerry, but close enough proximity to catch at my throat. It'd be so easy. All I'd have to do is tell Lennon I've changed my mind. He'd even say it's what he wants, because the guilt over his father's deeds is swallowing him whole.

I can't do that to him. I can't break or betray this bond between us, forged by a dragon, not even for my family. The flow of energy guides my words as I press at the tingle of power in my chest.

"I think it's a good idea for you and Kai to come here. Helena can protect you. But I'm going back to San Francisco with Lennon."

There's a sharp intake of breath. "You listen to me, madam. I'm your mother and you will obey me."

"Mum, I'm an adult now and a free woman on the Wayward Way. I do as I please, just like you did when you were my age. I won't abandon Lennon, especially after all he's done for our family. Besides, he needs me to defeat George Lau. Our family will never be safe until he's dead. Do you want to stay in the Beggar Abode for the rest of your life?"

"If it means we're all safe and together, then yes." Her voice wobbles and I know right well how much she wants to buy a caravan and return to the open road.

"Then it's settled. There's no other choice. I'm going to San Francisco with Lennon."

"Penny, no!"

I sigh and settle back, letting her pour all her frantic worries into my ear. It goes on for a while and I say, "Uh-huh," now and then, even though I'm not really listening. I concentrate on the hum of dragon energy, allowing it to fill my senses. Can it be transmitted through a phone line? I tap into the healing power of the Yin Pearl and transmit a tendril of courage through our connection.

Bridie gives a soft gasp. Then she's silent for a moment, "Though perhaps… perhaps you are right. I'm always jumping into the nearest bolt hole and that solves nothing."

"You were brilliant with Uncle Christy."

"Ha! Well, he had that coming. Trying to keep us captive like that. Hmph. And I certainly appreciate Tony Lau providing us with guards. I suppose we do owe him and Lennon some thanks. If only their father hadn't killed Gerry."

"Yeah," I whisper. There's no getting over that, but we can move past it so we can get on with our lives. I swallow hard. "Mum, I have to go. It's dinner time here and I'm really hungry."

"Yes, darling, go eat. You need to keep your strength up."

"Okay. I love you. Bye."

"I love you more than life, my darling girl!"

I hang up and stare at the phone. Bridie and Gerry were always making passionate declarations of love, hate, and everything in-between. Matthew was the voice of reason. I need to remind him not to get wound up in Bridie's hysteria.

I leave the carriage and take the lift to the ground floor of Greycoat Station. The common room is adjacent to the Haven, the homeless shelter the Beggars' use to camouflage their activities. Buffet stations serve food and drink at all hours because the Beggars work in shifts, prowling the streets, alleys, and underground twenty-four-seven. The windowless walls display the latest paintings found in dumpsters, abandoned in trains, or left on the street. They've accumulated quite a collection over the years, some by famous artists like Francis Bacon and Frida Kahlo, which are displayed in a gallery on a lower level. I'd love to show Lennon, but I'd have to ask Helena for permission, and I'm not sure she'd grant it.

I miss being that girl, the one who could skip through the Beggar Abode without a care in the world. She died with Gerry and she's not coming back, not even as a ghost.

I head for the supper buffet, where I load up on roasted beef, potatoes, and veg, along with a couple of crisp Yorkshire puddings, smothering it all in gravy. My mouth waters at the aroma, and my stomach rumbles as the dragon energy demands to be fed.

The mess is half-full of Beggar families enjoying their meal. I join Lennon, seated by himself at the table furthest from the door. He holds up a forkful of flaky pastry. "How is this pudding?"

I grin. "Think of it as a generic word."

"It's still not pudding," he mutters before shoving the fork in his mouth.

"You don't like it?"

"It's all right. Kinda plain."

"You're not eating it right." I cut a piece of Yorkshire pudding and sop up some gravy before taking a blissful bite.

He does the same and nods his head as he chews.

"How are the bachelor quarters?"

"Bachelor-y. I get to sleep in the same car as three guys who think I'm bullshit."

I roll my eyes. Typical Glory Road tactic. Maud demonstrates the Beggar Clan's dominance over the Two Dragon Clan by giving him inferior quarters. Exactly the kind of thing that made me choose to walk the Wayward Way.

A few minutes later, Matthew joins us, his plate also heavy-laden. He sits beside me without speaking. Disapproval at seeing me and Lennon together? Then he cuts a piece of roast beef, puts it in his mouth, and closes his eyes as he slowly chews. He swallows and sighs before saying, "That's the first solid food I've had in years."

Joy breaks through my wary gloom. "How does it taste?"

He shakes his head as if words fail him and goes on with his meal, savoring each of those first few bites. I wait a few moments before sliding the phone over to him. He sets down his fork. "So, you spoke to your mum, yeah?"

I nod. We exchange looks. Matthew nods. He knows. He always understood me better than Bridie or even Gerry.

"I'm glad you're staying," I say. "You, Bridie, and Kai. You'll be safe here."

Matthew chews around that. After swallowing, he says, "I've lived inside for too long. I need to walk free again, and I can't, not while George Lau is alive. I'm going with you."

"But if you go to SF, Bridie and Kai won't come to London."

"I know. But I don't think any of us are safer here or anywhere. Running away isn't the answer."

"My family is keeping them safe," Lennon volunteers. "I mean, safer than being on their own."

Matthew's eyes flick over at him. "We need to be on our own. That's how we live."

Another reminder that my family walks the Wayward Way of freedom, not the Glory Road of duty. Matthew doesn't know that Lennon also walks the Wayward Way, or he did until he was forced to become the Dragon Son.

Gareth arrives, holding two pints of beer. He hands one to Matthew before sitting beside him. "So, it's settled, yeah?"

Matthew nods. "Penny and I are going to San Francisco with the Dragon Son."

Gareth's lips spread thin. He takes a grim sip before saying, "What about Bridie and Kai?"

My heart aches for him. Gareth was part of our family and then, suddenly, we were gone. He's a battle-hardened warrior who knows life is full of peril, but that loss must still ache like an old wound that won't heal.

Matthew takes his hand. "We'll be back. I promise."

Gareth's eyes shine with sorrow. "That's what Bridie said when she took the kids to the States."

They need to talk. I pick up my plate and say to Lennon. "Let's get pudding."

Lennon rises quickly, doubtless tired of being the elephant in the middle of the room. When we get to the dessert buffet, his eyes narrow. One tray contains a plain, dense cake chock full of currants and sultanas. The other, a steamy yellow custard that smells heavenly. "That's pudding?"

I grin. I can't help it. "It's spotted dick."

"What?" He stares at me as if waiting for the punchline.

"Trust me, it's good."

I dish up two servings of cake, smothering them with custard before handing him his plate with a fork.

Instead of taking a bite, he asks, "Are you coming back here, too?"

How do I answer that? With the truth. It will hurt him, the same way it hurt Gareth, but I say it anyway.

"Yes."

Yes.

It's funny how a single word can punch you in the gut. I set down my steaming plate of not-pudding with a porno name. Why am I upset? I told Penny to stay here. I guess I thought when she said she's coming back to San Francisco with me, she meant for good. Obviously, she didn't. "So, when we're done, we're done?"

I want her to say no. Instead, she glares at me like I'm the one who wants to break up. "Did I say that?"

I shrug.

Her mouth pinches to one side like I'm annoying her. Then she nods for me to follow and walks away without looking back.

I hesitate because, you know, pride. Until I think about how shitty my life would be without her. I pick up my plate and follow her to an empty table at the far end of the room. We sit across from each other and poke at our dicks for a few moments without taking a bite. My phone buzzes in my pocket. I ignore it.

Steam rises from the yellow sauce on her plate as she

speaks. "I can't stay in San Francisco without my family. Where would I live? I don't make enough money to support myself, especially there."

I hadn't thought of that, and I should have. I know what it's like to be broke and homeless, but that would never happen to her. "You'd stay with me."

"At the *kongsi*? You think Tony will allow that?"

"I'm the Dragon Son, not him. I say what's allowed."

"Yeah, and it will be real fun for me, staying where I'm not welcome."

My stomach drops. Tony's mother made my mother feel unwelcome in our home. Even if Tony was on his best behavior, his silent disapproval would seep into everything, and I would hate him for it. Still, there has to be a way... "The art studio. You can stay there."

Frustration pinches her brow. "Okay, but Lennon, what am I doing there? Your family doesn't even want us to be friends, and your clan will never accept me."

"I just gotta get Tony to be the Dragon Son. Once that happens, I'm free. You and I can do... I don't know. Whatever."

"That won't be easy, and I don't want to be separated from my family while I'm waiting for it to happen. Do you understand?"

No. I'm pissed. She's betraying me. Us. Isn't our love worthy of her precious time? Why does her family have to come first?

Her arms fold. "Doesn't your family come first?"

I glance away from her sharp emerald gaze. I was careful not to project my thoughts, but she sensed them anyway. And she's right. I'd be expecting her to put my family first. To leave her family and wait around while I sort out the mess that is the Two Dragon Clan. I need her there, someone on my side. I want her to put her life on hold and miss out on the time she could spend with her family because I'm a selfish little shit.

My phone buzzes again. I flinch. Must be Tony. It's almost as if he's sensing this conversation and enforcing everything Penny is saying. I have to let her go. But what if she meets someone else?

There is no one else. There's only you.

I stare down at my cooling dick. It's both awesome and awful, being this close to someone. *Did you hear everything I thought?*

No. Just the last part. You could meet someone else, too, you know.

I look up and meet her wary gaze. *No. There's only you.*

Her chest rises and falls. I can sense the glow of the Yin Pearl under her shirt. *I need a home, and home for me isn't a place. It's in a caravan, on the open road, with my family. That's who I am.*

That's who she is. She's never told me anything different. When this is all over, I have to let her go. She'll always be my friend. She'll always have my heart. I have to learn to live with that. *I understand.*

Really?

Yeah. I heave a sigh. *When I ran away, I left Tony and Auntie Cat to deal with all the shit. That was a shitty thing for me to do.*

She shakes her head. *You were only fifteen and your parents had just been murdered.*

The way she sticks up for me, no matter what, it touches my heart. My true friend. I need to be her true friend, too, no matter how painful it will be for us to part.

It was still shitty. I need to go home and deal with it. I don't know how long that's going to take or what I'm going to do after, and, you're right, there's no point in you being there, waiting for me.

We stare at each other silently over our cooling dicks. Then Penny speaks aloud. "Remember that time we were on the beach and we talked about running away?"

How could I forget? The two of us, alone on the beach, kissing, coming so close, stopping. I'd told her I'd go traveling with her and I meant it.

Her voice softens. "When you're ready, let me know."

I'm so ready. I'd do it in a hot second if it weren't for… My phone buzzes against my thigh like a shock collar. What the hell does Tony want? I yank the phone from my pocket and stare at the screen.

> I spoke with Bridie Sparrow. She told me our
> father killed Penny's father. Why didn't you
> tell me?

I slump back in my chair, covering my mouth. Shit. Why can't I learn? I knew waiting to tell him wouldn't make things better. Why didn't I realize it could make things worse?

"What's wrong?" asks Penny.

I don't look at her as I turn the screen so she can read the text.

"You didn't tell him?"

"I wasn't ready." God, that sounds weak. She should totally dump me.

"It's all right. You didn't know they were going to talk." She pauses long enough for me to look up as her expression shifts from pragmatic to puzzled. "I wonder what they were talking about."

"Us, probably."

"Maybe…" Her voice trails off as she pulls her phone out. She winces at the screen. "It's Bridie."

Penny

The table feels like a gulf between us, full of uneaten spotted dick and regret. The custard smell has become sickly sweet and gags my throat. We turn our backs to each other because it's too weird dealing with Tony and Bridie while being face-to-face.

As I stare at the missed call notification gathering my thoughts, my phone rings again. I tap the screen and make the choice to play stupid. "Mum, what's up?"

"Tony Lau called." The crisp outrage in her voice makes me bite my lip. "He said that after what happened in London today, Kai and I should move into the *kongsi*. I thanked him and said I thought it would be awkward, considering everything. He said he didn't know what I meant, which I thought was heartless, until I spelled it out." She groans. "That was dreadful. Why didn't Lennon tell him their father murdered Gerry?"

I glance over my shoulder at Lennon, deep in his regretful conversation. "He wanted to wait until he got home so he could tell Tony in person."

"Now isn't the time for delicate sensibilities. Not when

we're all in such terrible danger."

I take a hesitant breath. "I know it's awkward, but maybe you should plant in the *kongsi*. It's a lot safer there."

She snorts. "Not bloody likely. I already turned down Jeremiah."

"Jeremiah?"

"News travels fast on the Crossroads. You and Lennon are becoming infamous, like Bonnie and Clyde."

Partners in crime. That's how we see ourselves. Is that how everyone sees us now? "When did Jeremiah call?"

"Right after I spoke with you. He said Kai and I need safe haven after your exploits. I told him to get stuffed." Bridie snorts. "The nerve of him! As if he wouldn't deliver us back into Christy's clutches."

"Good for you, Mum. We're well shot of Jeremiah and Uncle Christy, but he's right in one sense. You and Kai need to be someplace safer than our apartment. Tony doesn't want to crimp us. He'll want us to rattle once everything is done."

"True." She gusts out a sigh. "I guess the *kongsi* is our only choice, but having to live under the cutty-eye of that uppish Tony…"

I try sounding cheerful. "Give him your own cutty-eye, Mum."

She won't be cheered. "How strange and awful that we must depend on the sons of Gerry's killer for help."

"Don't think of them like that. It's not fair."

"I know it's not fair, but I think what I think, and that's all there is to it."

I don't argue because what's the point? I let her get off the phone so she can call Matthew with the news.

"What's cutty-eye?" asks Lennon.

I turn to face him. "It's Strowler for stink-eye."

His face goes owlish. "I wasn't eavesdropping."

"I know. What did Tony say?"

"That I need to grow up, and it's my fault that Bridie refuses to stay at the *kongsi*."

I wince. Tony's right. Lennon needs to grow up and so do I, but we're both only eighteen. Don't we get more time? Maybe if our situation wasn't so dire, we'd have that time. Instead, we frustrate everyone and ourselves.

"Well, the good news is I got Bridie to agree to stay there."

Lennon exhales with relief. "Is that what the stink-eye was about?"

"Cutty-eye and yeah."

Lennon and I say little after that except good night. Too much has happened too quickly. I need to sleep. I go to Matthew and Gareth, still deep in conversation, to bid them good night. Both hug me tight and gaze at me with worried eyes, reminding me what it's like to have a father. I mean, a real father, one who places their hopes for the future on you. It's wonderful and awful because it warms my heart, but also makes me realize I can't live up to that hope if I'm with Lennon.

I'm relieved Matthew continues his conversation with Gareth. When I get to our carriage, I close the door and heave a sigh of relief, grateful to be alone. The interior is a lot like the caravans I'd lived in all my life until we moved to San Francisco. There's a kitchenette, a bathroom, curtained bunk beds, and a private bedroom. A row of the original seats serve as a sofa.

Unlike our caravan, there's an abundance of hot water, so I take a long shower, washing away the grit of two continents. So much has happened in so little time. My body should ache, but it's my heart and soul that are full of pain. The steamy water takes the edge off my anxiety. Everyone I care about is safe for the moment. I need to take some comfort in that so I can sleep.

The bathroom is stocked with all I need except one vital

thing: fresh clothes. My nose wrinkles at the stench of body odor as I tug my T-shirt over my head. I need to talk to Maud about that in the morning. Then I climb into the top bunk, which had always been mine by right of seniority. Kai had the lower bunk, Gerry had the cabover, and Matthew and Bridie slept in the bedroom. When Gerry would follow his fancy, he'd stay out all night. He brought no one home except Gareth. Things became tight when they finally plighted their troth, so they decided to buy their own caravan…

I suck in a painful breath. Dwelling in the beautiful past won't help me sleep. I draw the curtain and nestle into the unfamiliar bedding. Everything feels scratchy, even though it's not. Maybe it's the constant rumble of trains itching at my nerves. I close my eyes and place my hand over the Yin Pearl. Its soothing aura radiates through my body, relaxing me into a slumber.

I dream of an isolated cove on the Irish coast. Stars shine like glitter splashed across a black velvet cloth. Turgid waves lap at the rocky shore and the air smells of salt and ruin. Wet sand sinks beneath my feet as I stride toward a glowing green light that appears in the cliff's crevice. It looks like the shell of energy that surrounded me and Lennon when we rode on Jade Dragon's back. I reach out to touch it and my hand goes right through. Another hand closes around mine. I gasp and almost tug away, except the hand feels familiar. Loving. I allow myself to be drawn through the shell. It shimmers around me, making my skin tingle.

I step into a huge cavern glowing green and white, though there's no source of light. Stalactites hang like jagged crystal daggers from the porous stone ceiling. The air is moist and warm and the walls glisten with the constant trickle of water. My feet rest not on stone but on glittering gold coins. Jewels, pearls, trinkets of all kinds spill off huge mounds of treasure looted from sunken vessels.

This must be Master Stoorworm's lair, which means I'm somewhere beneath the Irish Sea. I twist around, searching for my reptilian forefather, but he's nowhere to be seen. Only my real father, still holding my hand.

Gerry.

He stands before me, barefoot, wearing skinny jeans, his favorite leather jacket, and favorite shirt. Around his neck, a dragon pearl thrums with power. His lips lift in that devilish grin. "Surprise, Penny Lane."

"Da!" I move to embrace him.

He shakes his head and steps back, kissing my hand before letting go.

I wake with a sharp gasp and press my hands against the pounding of my heart. The sound of a rumbling train assures me I'm still in the Abode. After a few deep breaths to calm myself, I rub my forehead. Perhaps Gerry's presence still lingers, but why would he send me such a dream? Maybe he knows, in my heart of hearts, that I wish it were he that swallowed the Yin Pearl and made it out alive. I love Matthew so much and I'm happy for Bridie and Kai. Is it selfish to wish for that same happiness for me and Gareth? But if Gerry were alive, Matthew would be dead. How could I stand that after having him back again? That's what Gerry was doing in my dream, holding a mirror to my soul.

Thanks a lot, Da.

I sit up, pulling aside the curtain to get some air, and see Matthew sitting on the sofa, staring at the telly with a quizzical frown. The BBC News is on, muted, with subtitles. On the Crossroads, we don't much care what happens in the Bleater world. Still, three years is a long time to go with no information at all.

I slide out of the bunk bed. Matthew turns as my feet hit the floor. His frown becomes concerned. "Did I wake you, love?"

I shake my head. An impulse takes hold of me to tell him about my dream and I struggle against it. As much as I want to share it with him, I don't want to hurt his feelings. I glance at the screen. "Are they still talking about the shooting?"

He nods. "They don't think it's a terrorist attack anymore. They're saying the sniper had a grudge against the hospital. He left a suicide note in his hotel room."

Planted by George Lau's minions. Or did he use the Wisdom Pearl to persuade the sniper to write his own death note? I shudder. "Did anyone die in the attack?"

"Some tourists were wounded, but the only one who died was the gunman."

Killed by us. Me and Lennon. I don't want to think about it. I wish I could climb into Matthew's lap like I had as a child, wrap my arms around him, and rest my head on his chest while he stroked my hair and sang softly, but I'm too old now. Still, I go to the couch and curl up beside him. I smell beer and something else. Soap and shampoo. "All right?"

He points the remote at the TV, turning it off. "I guess. I had a few pints with Gareth. We talked for a long time. Then I wandered around for a while. Took a shower in the gym. Wandered some more." He ducks his head. "I'm afraid to go to sleep. Afraid I won't wake up. That I'll go back to how I was."

I sit up straight, tugging on his arm. "You won't. But even if you do, Lennon and I can heal you, so don't be scared."

"I know. My mind tells me that, but my heart..." He rubs his chest as if to massage away the ache. "I missed you, Penny Lane, all of you. I was in a coma, but I sensed the passage of time. It must've been the Yin Pearl. I could sense what was happening around me, but not in a solid way." He frowns. "It's hard to explain. I need to tell you about the pearl."

"It can wait. We both need to sleep."

"Sleep," he breathes out the word. "I haven't slept in years."

My heart aches, too, for him, trapped in that purgatory, neither alive nor dead, thanks to his parents and their schemes. "Go to bed. It'll be all right."

"All right. You take the room. I can sleep in the bunk."

I shake my head. "The bunk makes this feel like home for me."

He smiles before he stands and kisses the top of my head. "Good night, Penny Lane."

"Good night, Ba."

Ba is Cantonese for father. Matthew was Ba, Gerry was Da, and Gareth was Pa during that short, sweet interval when life blessed me with three fathers.

I climb back into my bunk. It feels cozier now that I know Matthew is here. It's after midnight and the trains have stopped running. I think of how Gerry's spirit helped me escape the Nest so Lennon and I could rescue Matthew. This is what he wanted and I'm happy. I close my eyes and whisper, "Good night, Da."

I feel the brush of his fingers on my cheek as I fall asleep.

Penny

When I awaken again, it's to the rumbling vibration of a nearby train. I check my phone. It's almost eleven. I close my eyes and try to get a sense of whether all that sleep did my body any good. Aside from a bit of grogginess, I feel the steady thrum of dragon energy flowing through me. My phone vibrates. I check the screen and see Lennon's name.

Hey. I just woke up.

Me, too. I guess we were pretty tired.

Yeah. Wanna do brunch?

Lol. Yes! Meet you in a few.

As I climb out of the bunk, I hear Matthew's and Bridie's voices. The bedroom door is opened a crack, but I give a warning knock before poking my head in. He's nestled among the pillows, staring at the phone, looking more relaxed than last night.

"Good morning," I mouth.

"Hold on, it's Penny," he says to the screen before smiling up at me. "Good morning, love." He blinks with childlike wonderment. "I'm awake."

My smile almost breaks my face. "Yes, you are. I'm going to get breakfast. Want to come with?"

"Not yet. I could be a while with your mother."

"I can wait."

"That's all right. Go eat. I'll join you later."

A guilty twinge squeezes my chest as I leave the car. I'd offered to stay not to be nice, but because I wanted to throw him off the scent with Lennon, and it worked. I'm a shit daughter. Well, that's been true for a while now. Might as well own it.

As I enter the common room, I spot Lennon sitting in what's become our spot. As our eyes meet, a surge of heat passes between us that has nothing to do with dragons. I feel my cheeks color and I look away so no one will notice.

Since Beggars keep odd hours, the breakfast buffet is always stocked, meaning Lennon and I really can have brunch. I dish up sausage, eggs, stewed tomatoes, and toast, and pour a big mug of coffee. Then I carry my tray across the room, trying not to be too obvious as I make a beeline for him. As I sit, our feet touch under the table and a jolt of electricity moves through me. Does he feel it, too?

"Hi," we say at the same time.

I look down at my food. Why does this feel so strange? It's still us. Me and him. Things have changed. Lots of things. But we haven't. Have we?

"I had a weird dream last night," I finally say.

Owl Boy appears, giving a sage nod. "One power of the Yin Pearl is prophetic dreams."

"You mean, like, dreams about the future?"

"I guess. The manuals for the pearls have been lost for

almost two hundred years, so no one really knows anymore. Why? What'd you dream about?"

"Gerry."

"Oh." He ducks his head. "Why was it weird?"

I glance over my shoulder before whispering, "Don't tell Matthew, but I dreamed Gerry was wearing the Yin Pearl." I sigh. "So, it can't be prophetic. He was a part of my past, not my future."

"Except our future is all about the past."

He's right. I sip my coffee and chew around a piece of toast while I think. I can't make the connection.

Lennon digs into his eggs in owlish silence before speaking again. "Maybe the dream needs to be interpreted by someone else."

That makes sense. "Bridie has that gift. Sometimes, instead of busking, she'd set up a table and offer to read palms and interpret dreams. Gerry would have a shell game going nearby. Matthew and Kai would strum their guitars and I'd be dancing." I duck my head. Those were good times. How did I not see them as the best of times?

"Maybe tell Bridie your dream?"

I shake my head. "She'll think I want Gerry back instead of Matthew. I think subconsciously I do and I feel shitty enough about that without bringing her into it."

He shrugs. "You can't help what you dream."

"I know, or what I feel, but..." My voice trails off as Helena enters the common area. My shoulders tense. I should pretend not to see her, but I can't help admiring her style. She's wearing combat boots, black-and-white striped socks, a flouncy plaid skirt with frayed, uneven layers, and a long, black wool sweater with patched elbows, clasped from her waist to her neck with an assortment of buttons. Day-glo scrunchies and a ring of colorful hair clips hold the wayward strands of her unruly curls, forming a fitting crown for a Beggar Queen.

She winds past the crowded tables, amiably nodding as her subjects greet her.

"What is it?" asks Lennon, his back turned to her.

"Mad Maud's coming over. Don't look."

He turns and looks. He and Helena lock eyes before he twists back around.

"I said don't look," I hiss.

"I can't not look. What if she pulls a shiv on me?"

That's funny enough that we both sputter with laughter.

Queen Maud is not amused as she joins us. She nods at Lennon. "Dragon Son."

He nods back. "Beggar Chief."

She turns her attention to me. "Done eating?"

I hesitate, but she's eyeing my empty plate, so all I can do is nod.

"Come with me."

Pants. Here we go. Doubtless, Bridie sent Helena to give me 'the talk.' I manage not to roll my eyes. "See you later," I say to Lennon

He gives a tight shrug. "I'll be here."

I keep my arms crossed tight as Helena leads me out of the mess hall. I follow her through a series of corridors, our silence broken only by the hum of the metro and the tapping of her cane. My brain chews through responses to her likely questions. What I really want to do is shout, 'Bugger off!', but that's not something I can say to Mad Maud. When I was a kid, I wanted to be her. I kind of still do, except I don't want to lead or follow. I want to go my own way.

We stop at a door stenciled with the word RUMMAGE. I can't help smiling and she can't help smiling back.

"Thought we'd go on a little shopping spree," she says with a wink before touching a keycard to the lockbox.

"Okay." My arms unfold and I clasp my hands before me as if she's opening the gate to Paradise.

Rummage is a private thrift store run by the Beggar Clan. It's open only to Hearth clients, who use vouchers to purchase clothes and other goods. It's also used by the Beggars when they need "new" clothes. Helena used to take me shopping here, and we'd swap fashion tips while rummaging through the aisles.

Bridie hated it. She'd tell me, "Strowlers dress flash, not trash." Young as I was, I knew what she meant. Settled people look down on Strowlers and other traveling people as if we're homeless tramps, so we tend to wear bright, expensive clothing to display our wealth, even if we have none.

I didn't care, then or now. I want to be like Helena and pull together an amazing fashion statement out of nothing.

"We have the place to ourselves," says Helena as she turns on the lights. In keeping with Beggar Clan security, the store has no windows, and the single outside door is heavily tinted and barricaded with iron bars. "I figured you could use a change of clothes."

"I do. Thanks." I pause. "So do Matthew and Lennon."

"I know. I'll have them brought here."

"Why didn't you ask Lennon to come with us?"

"I thought we could shop together, just us, for old time's sake."

She's definitely reeling me in. Two can play at that game.

"Fun." I go to the nearest rack and start sorting through the dresses. Before long, I find a purple long-sleeved skater dress patterned with glittery silver moons and stars. I yank it out and hold it against me while staring in a mirror. "I'll take this one."

"It suits you," she says with a smile.

"Thanks." I fold it over my arm. "I'll need leggings to go with it. And other things."

"Take whatever you want."

I pick out a brown corduroy pinafore before moving to the next rack, where I snag a ribbed jumper with pink, blue, green, and brown stripes. I hold them against me as I look in the mirror. So cute. Behind me, I spot a rainbow scarf that looks handknit. Insta-buy, so to speak. I wrap it around my neck before sorting through the T-shirts.

Helena follows me, hesitation on her face as she searches for the right words. It's kind of funny when you think about it. She's one of the most powerful people on the Crossroads, and she doesn't know what to say to a teenager. Is that what happens when you get older? Do you lose the ability to say what you mean? I don't have that problem.

"Have you ever been in love?" I ask.

The look on her face. Has she ever looked that panicked when she faced down a well-armed opponent? I don't think so.

"Yes," she finally answers. "Once."

"What was he like?"

She shakes her head as if words fail her.

"Fit? Flash? Bonny?"

"I suppose. All those things."

"So, it didn't work out?"

"No."

"Why not?"

"I'd rather not say. It's private."

"Private," I repeat with raised eyebrows. I didn't even have to try. She walked right into that. I pick out an oversized Boy London T-shirt that will work as nightgown and head for the trousers.

Her mouth puckers as she shadows me. "Sometimes things don't work out between people, no matter how much love there is. Sometimes you can't overcome the obstacles."

"Were you in different clans?"

"No. That would've made it even harder."

"Gareth and Gerry were in different clans. So are Bridie and Matthew."

"Yes, and it's always been very hard for them."

"That never stopped them." I grab a pair of jeans and some leggings and head for the dressing room. I don't mean to sound heartless, but if she wasn't willing to stand up for love…

"It was a woman," Helena says to my back. "I was in love with a woman."

My eyes widen as I spin around. "You're a lesbian?"

"Bisexual," she corrects. "I fancy men as well, but Nance, she was special. Strong. Tough as nails. We were stationed together in Afghanistan. She's part of the Birmingham Beggar Clan."

"A Brummie?" That's almost more surprising.

She grins. "Aye. We tried making a go of it when we finished our tour of duty, but we're both ambitious. I wanted to be Mad Maud of London and she wanted to be Brummie Maud. So…"

"So, you gave up on each other?"

"No, I wouldn't say that." Her tone becomes defensive. "We realized we couldn't be together and… and…"

"Gave up?"

Helena looks flummoxed. This isn't going her way, but I don't want to go for the kill. It's hard being gay on the Cross-roads. It makes me love her even more. "Sorry. I don't mean to be a bitch about it. And sorry it didn't work out for you and Nance. She sounds cracker."

"She was. She still is."

"Is she Brummie Maud yet?"

"No. She's waiting for the next election."

"Or maybe she's waiting for something else. Just saying." I don't move because I know there's more she wants to say. Might as well let her say it.

She inhales before letting it out. "Penny, however much you think you love this boy; it can't work. You can't change who he is."

"I don't want to change him. Who he is, is who I love."

She continues as if I hadn't spoken. "Even if he wasn't the Dragon Son, his father killed your father. Nothing will change that. It will always come between you."

"Why?"

Her brow wrinkles. "Why?"

"Yeah. Why will it always come between us?"

She sputters before answering. "Because… because it will. That's how people are."

I shrug. "Not all people. Not us."

"Oh, Penny," she sighs out my name.

"What Lennon and I want most in the world is to keep our families safe. That includes you and Gareth. If you'd all just leave us alone and stop interfering, it will make things a lot easier for us." That comes out more forceful than I mean it to be. Helena looks taken aback. She still sees me as a frivolous fifteen-year-old who loves dancing and fashion. I'm still that girl, but I'm also something more and they need to understand that.

"When all is done, will you continue using this power you have with the Dragon Son?" she asks quietly.

I reply without hesitation. "No. That's not an option. I'm not part of the Two Dragon Clan."

She looks relieved, but that's only because she doesn't realize that Lennon plans to give both pearls to Tony after he convinces him to be the Dragon Son. Then we'll walk the Wayward Way together, regardless of approval.

After all, I already have the blessing of Gerry's ghost. All I need to do is convince everyone else.

Lennon

About an hour after Mad Maud takes Penny away, this dude named Clive comes to get me. I'm sharing the same boxcar with him and two other young guys with old man names. Terrence and Wilfred. I kid you not. They spend most of their time either arguing over which is the best branch of the military to join, or bitching and moaning about having to wait until they're twenty-one to enlist. I can't think of anything I'd like to do less than enlist…

No, wait. There is one thing. I'd much rather join the army than be the Dragon Son. But here I am.

I don't ask Clive where we're going, since I'm pretty sure he won't tell me. So, it's a pleasant surprise when he leads me into a thrift store next to the station. It's my lucky day because someone my size has discarded all their emo gear. I load up on black jeans, band T-shirts, and a black hoodie with a skeletal ribcage printed on the front and spinal cord on the back. On the way out, I grab a pair of cheap earbuds to complete the look.

Clive escorts me back to the boxcar and tells me to wait there. As soon as he shuts the door, I shred my clothes which still smell faintly of dragon. Sort of like a turtle, but not that bad. Just not great. I pull on the skinniest, most shredded jeans, a Panic! at the Disco T-shirt, and the hoodie. Then I go into the bathroom and use water and my fingers to comb my hair over one eye. I look emo as hell and that's the idea. No one takes an emo kid seriously or sees him as a threat, or as someone who can blow them away with a whisper.

There's a knock on the door. Before I can say, 'come in' or 'fuck off', it slides open and Mad Maud steps inside. Clive, who was obviously standing guard outside, slides it closed behind her.

I sigh audibly, because here we go.

"Hi," I say because she's just standing there, looking at me. She's got an unwavering stare that reminds me of Tony. Maybe that's what you need to be a Crossroads leader.

"Dragon Son," she finally says, "your passport is sorted. You're now on record as having legally entered the UK. You can leave whenever you want."

I manage not to flinch. Is she kicking me out? "If it's okay with you, I'll leave when Penny and Matthew are ready to go."

"You seek refuge within this Abode?"

"Um, yeah." I don't add 'obviously', but it's implied in an emo way.

Her cane slides off her shoulder, hitting the floor with a heavy tap. "Jeremiah Walks Long tells me you ran away from home after your parents died."

What's that got to do with anything?

"That you took refuge in his Abode. Because you were a child, no debt of honor needed to be repaid."

Sure.

"Now that you're an adult and have taken refuge with us again, we cannot ignore your debt."

There it is.

She leans on her cane with both hands, pausing as if

waiting for me to say something. When I don't, she takes a breath. "I realize I owe you gratitude for healing Matthew."

I shake my head. "I didn't do it for you."

"You did it for Penny."

"Her and her family, yeah."

Mad Maud's eyes narrow in on me. "What have you done to her?"

I say, "What do you mean?" Even though I know exactly what she means.

"Gareth told me what you and she can do together."

"Oh, that. Yeah." I shrug. "Clan secret. You know how that goes."

She's totally going to kick me out. I can see it in her eyes, calculating the worth of keeping me as opposed to shoving me out the front door.

"What happened to Penny and her family is the fault of your clan, and it is unforgivable. My brother lost his husband because of your father."

My chest tightens. Mad Maud knows how to twist the knife. Thing is, I can't feel worse about my family. I'm already there. I speak in a hoarse whisper, "You want payback from me for what my father did?"

"I want you to stop seeing Penny," she answers in a rush of words.

I shake my head. "No."

I know she wants to take this further, but she can't. On the Crossroads, children don't pay for the sins of their parents. I mean, sure, you'll be shunned and treated like shit, but you don't have to physically pay. Just mentally and emotionally, for the rest of your fucking life.

"Why won't you let her go?"

I roll my eyes. Adults. I guess I'm one now, too, but still. "I'm not keeping her. She can do what she wants. If she doesn't want to hang out with me, cool. I mean, yeah, I'd be upset and whatever, but I'm not some loser holding onto someone who doesn't want to be with me." I scoff and cross my arms. "Who does that?"

She clenches the top of her cane. For a moment, I wonder if she's going to whack me with it. Her eyes are mild, though, and she sighs through her nose. "So, you'll let her go?"

"I just said I'm not holding onto her."

"But she won't leave you."

I groan. "What do you want from me?"

"For you to convince her to leave you."

I shake my head. "You act like you're so concerned about Penny, but you don't trust her. You don't think she has a mind of her own. Well, guess what? I already tried to convince her. It didn't work. So, done. Think of something else, some other way to punish me for being Michael Lau's son."

"You think that's what I'm doing?"

"Obviously."

Her face tightens with her glare. "I want revenge, but I can't take it out on you. I'd rather take it out on your clan."

"What do you mean? You mean, like, on my brother. It wasn't his fault."

"Not you. Not your brother. Your entire clan."

"How?"

The glare disappears as her face becomes a cold, formal mask. "I want you to swear that no Dragon Son will seek to be the head of the Crossroads ever again."

I squint. "You mean, forever?"

"Yes."

Honestly, that sounds great to me. Being head of the Crossroads has been a curse to my family and my clan. It ruined us. Still, like Prince says about forever, that's a mighty long time. And I have to face Tony again, not her. "How about a compromise?"

She tilts her head. "I'm listening."

"How about for a hundred years?"

Her lips thin as she thinks. I'm afraid she's going to say, 200 years, and then I'll say 150 and she'll say…

"Very well."

I feel my face go blank. "Great. Um, you wanna do it now?"

"Yes."

"Okay. Um, how? Is there something I'm supposed to do, or say, or what?"

Mad Maud's long sigh deflates her. "There's no joy in this for me."

"Was there supposed to be?"

She gives a mirthless laugh. "I don't know." She reaches into the depths of her skirt and pulls out her phone. She taps the screen and holds it out to record me. "Just say the words."

Talk about being put on the spot. "Okay. So, I, Lennon… Paul Lau, the Dragon Son, to repay my debt to the Beggar Clan, I solemnly swear that no Dragon Son will try being the head of the Crossroads for the next hundred years. On my honor and the honor of the Two Dragon Clan. Is that good?"

She taps the phone again. "That's good."

"Do you feel good?"

"No." She shoves the phone back in her pocket. The cane swings back up to her shoulder. "Someday, you'll learn that life isn't about feeling good."

"Really? I hope not."

She squeezes her thumb and forefinger into a narrow opening. "I was this close to throwing you out of the Abode, and I would've, but I know Penny and Matthew would go with you."

"You hate me that much?"

"I don't hate you at all. I want revenge, and nothing will give it to me."

I don't know about that. I think she got some decent

revenge. Maybe she'd think so, too, if she got to watch me tell Tony about my oath. Speaking of which.

"Can you do me a favor?" I ask. Mad Maud's brow rises, but she doesn't tell me to fuck off, so I continue. "Before you play that for whoever - Jeremiah, I guess - Can you wait until I get back to San Francisco? I want to tell my brother in person."

"I'll tell Jeremiah and no one else. I guarantee our silence until after you defeat your uncle. We don't want to cause defections among your followers."

That works. "Thanks. Though you know my uncle won't honor our agreement if I lose."

"Another reason I won't kick you out of the Abode." She slides open the door and strolls away, her cane tapping on the cement platform like a drip from a faucet.

With allies like her, who needs enemies?

Clive doesn't return, so I'm alone in the boxcar. I exhale and stretch out on the bottom bunk bed assigned to me. I realize I'm not really alone. I already checked the SpyNot app and I'm totally being watched from every angle, except in the toilet. Decent of them. I close my eyes rather than stare at the wooden slats of the bed above mine and think about Dad.

Now that I've killed someone, maybe I understand better. Dad didn't know who Gerry and Matthew were. He was attacking thieves, stealing our clan's lost treasures. Treasures he'd kill to protect. I might've done the same thing in his place. Maybe that's what's going to come between me and Penny. Deep down she must know, like I do, that he had no choice. Just like when we pushed the sniper off the building or when we channeled Matthew's illness into the other assassin. We knew nothing about those guys. What if Uncle George forced them to act against us? We still didn't have any choice.

That's all well and good if it's not your father at either end of the gun.

My phone buzzes. I yank it out of my pocket and stare at the screen.

> I can't have dinner with you tonight. Sorry.
> Helena invited me and Matthew to a private
> dinner with her and Gareth.

I squeeze the phone to keep from texting back immediately. I want to tell Penny not to go. That Mad Maud is a bitch who's trying to keep us apart. In other words, I want to prove Mad Maud right and that her accusations against me were justified. I grit my teeth before texting back.

> Ok. I'm gonna get some coffee. Join me?

> I can't. Matthew asked me to go shopping
> with him at Rummage. Then we're going to
> call Bridie and Kai to say goodnight.

So, Matthew's in on it, too. Like that's a big surprise.

> Ok. Have fun.

> Are you all right?

> I'll survive. Being here is weird.

> I know. We'll meet for breakfast no matter
> what, ok?

> Ok.

I smile before I send my heart. Mad Maud and all of them can try, but they can't take us away from us.

After that, I hunker down in the common room, earbuds in, staring at my phone like the sullen teen I am. Tony calls and I loudly tell him I can't talk because people are listening, which is 100% true. I watch music videos and graffiti tutorials among other random shit, and make sure anyone who wants to can see my screen.

Spending the day as a poser is exhausting and I go to bed early, although I know I won't be able to sleep. So, I close my eyes and take slow, deep breaths until that emo part of me fades and I can feel the flow of my chi. I flow with it, though my body, finding my rhythm of being, and with another breath, I flow into the Yang Pearl.

The energy surrounds me like water in a nameless, depthless ocean. I float amidst waves that are both fiery hot and icy cold. Then I realize that's not the water and I'm not alone.

Why are you here? asks Jade Dragon.

I can't sleep. Where are you?

Here.

Oh. Okay.

Hatchlings require rest to restore their chi. Go to sleep.

I drift out of the Yang Pearl and into a slumber.

I'm home. Not the *kongsi*. I'm standing at the end of the pier outside my art studio. Fog covers the San Francisco Bay like a damp, gray blanket. It's comforting, familiar. I close my eyes and listen for the moan of the foghorns and the yelping of the sea lions. Instead, I hear footsteps. I turn and see this guy strolling toward me through the mist. He's wearing skinny jeans, a maroon shirt, a tight brown leather jacket with the sleeves rolled up, and a colorful scarf tied around his neck. He's got a curly mop of black hair, thick eyebrows, and the bluest eyes I've ever seen. It can only be one person, so I say his name.

"Gerry?"

He nods and smiles. "All right."

I'm not sure how to answer, so I shake my head. "I'm sorry my dad shot you."

He shrugs. "Not your fault, mate. Or his. Hurt like hell, though."

We're about the same height, which surprises me. I guess he always seemed larger than life to me. "Don't you hate me? Aren't you going to order me to stay away from Penny?"

He throws back his head and laughs, though the fog muffles the sound. "Penny makes up her own mind. Fuck the patriarchy, yeah?"

"Yeah." Wow. He's as cool as I'd thought.

His smile fades as he glances over his shoulder. "You gotta be strong. You won't win if you let them hold you back."

"What? Who?"

The fog envelopes him and he's gone.

I awaken with a gasp. I can almost feel the mist clinging to my skin. It takes a moment to internalize it wasn't real. All that's left is a slight headache and a strong desire to see Penny.

Penny

I find Gerry lounging in the atrium, on a bench next to the waterfall. The mist dampens his black hair, loosening the curls. He opens those eyes of heartbreaking blue and says, "There's our girl."

I sit beside him. "Do you ever regret having me, Da?"

Those eyes widen. "Why would you think such a thing?"

I shrug. "Dunno. I guess, because I made you feel trapped."

"You made me feel like I belonged. I'm a mad bastard, and I regret a lot of things, but not you. Never you."

I take a deep breath of contentment. We sit together in companionable silence until Gareth walks by. He looks past us as if we're not there, his face intent and his eyes with that lingering sadness.

"Da," I shake his arm. "Why don't you tell Gareth we're here?"

He stares after him, his eyes filled with a similar sorrow. "He knows, but he can't see."

"Why not?"

Gerry's lips part as if he's about to answer. Then he sits up abruptly. "She's here."

"Who?" I glance around. "Helena?"

He shakes his head. "Her. She's here."

"Where?"

He presses the pinprick spot on my chest. Then presses the same spot on his own. "She sings everything into being."

"What are you on about, Da?"

He smiles, shakes his head, and closes his eyes. A dragon pearl reappears around his neck, casting a greenish-red glow.

I awaken with a gasp, followed by a disappointed whimper at finding myself in the carriage bunk bed. Gerry was right there. We were together. It felt so natural. I close my eyes and go over the details, so I don't forget. *She sings everything into being.* What does that mean? I could ask Bridie, but not without setting her off. I roll over, wishing it was morning so I could tell Lennon.

I awaken again to the buzz of a text message. Not from Lennon. Helena is inviting me and Matthew to a private breakfast. I roll my eyes. She'll do anything to keep me and Lennon apart. I want to refuse, but that's not something you can do when taking refuge in another clan's gaff. Still, if she tries that game at lunch, I will say no.

Surprisingly, she doesn't. Maybe she has better things to do, as Beggar Chief of bloody London, than keep two teenagers apart.

I get a sandwich for lunch with nothing on the side but coffee. Looks like my dragon appetite has finally died down. Does that mean the power has gone as well? I still feel the pinprick of pain, but that's about it. After shooting Lennon a text to let him know I'm here, I take a bite of my sandwich, savoring the taste of cheddar cheese with proper Branston Pickle. They sell it in the States, but it doesn't taste the same.

Lennon shows up at our table with new clothes and an owlish expression. I squint at his Black Parade T-shirt as he settles beside me with his tray.

"What?" he asks.

"I didn't figure you for a My Chemical Romance fan."

He shrugs. "They're okay. I like your dress."

"Thanks." I'm wearing the purple skater dress with leggings, boots, and a scarf. Not the most stunning fashion statement, but I'm trying to keep a low profile, unlike Lennon with his Emo Boi look. Maybe we should've coordinated. Then again, sometimes the best way to blend in is to stand out and play with people's expectations. Clever boy.

"How was dinner and, um, breakfast?" he asked.

I shrug, because I don't want to admit I loved being with Matthew, Gareth, and Helena again. I missed them terribly and being with them filled some holes in my heart. "All right. It was only bad yesterday when Helena took me shopping. That was just an excuse to tell me to stay away from you."

"She told me the same thing."

Of course she did. Why does she think it's her right to interfere? "When?"

"After I went shopping." He takes a bite of his ham and egg sandwich.

"What happened?"

He chews and swallows before saying, "Nothing."

"You expect me to believe that?"

"No. It's just…" He sighs and sets down the sandwich. "It'll piss you off and I don't need trouble with Mad Maud."

"Tell me."

His mind brushes against mine, and I let him in. He tells me and he's right. It bloody well pisses me off.

"That's bollocks," I say aloud, slamming my hand on the table, making our trays rattle. "She can't do that. I'm going to go talk to her." I stand.

"Penny." He says my name in such a way, so deadly serious, that I sit back down. "It's between me and her, and it's done."

I whisper because I'm too upset to use Silent Speech. "It's not fair. She's asking too much."

"It's a tactic. The Beggar Clan sees me as a threat. They need to neutralize me without killing me because my uncle is a bigger threat. This is their chance to rule the Crossroads. They're welcome to it."

He says that now, but how will he feel a year from now? Helena must've dumped a load of guilt on him, enough to make him swear such an oath. What kind of honor is there in that?

Lennon picks at the crust of his sandwich and mutters, "Tony's gonna kill me, though."

"Did you tell him?"

"Not yet. I got Mad Maud to agree to keep her mouth shut until I do."

"That was big of her."

"It was the least she could do."

Literally. I'm still fuming, but what can I do? I sip my coffee, since it matches my bitter mood. Helena, Tony, Jeremiah, Bridie, they need to realize we're all on the same side. Playing clan politics won't win the day against George Lau.

Lennon keeps picking at his sandwich without eating. Looks like his dragon appetite is gone, too. "So, I wanted to tell you. Last night, I had a dream about Gerry."

Coffee burns down my throat as I swallow hard. "You did? What did you dream?"

"We were on a pier, and I said I was sorry, and he said it's not my fault." He pauses and chews his lip as if biting back more words. Then he looks me in the eye. "He told me you're your own person, that you do what you want, and fuck the patriarchy."

I press my hand to my heart because that sounds so like him. "Did he say anything else?"

"Yeah," he breathes out the word. "That I need to be strong

and not let anyone hold me back." He shakes his head. "It felt so real, like, when I woke up, I couldn't believe he wasn't still there."

"I dreamed about him again last night. I felt the same way." Should I tell him about Gerry's ghost visiting me during Samhain? I've told no one because it was strange and private, and I know if I talk about it, I'll cry. Plus, part of me wants to believe it wasn't real, that Gerry's spirit has passed on despite him being buried at the crossroads by his wicked family.

"Do you believe in ghosts?" I ask.

Lennon shrugs. "I guess. I mean, my parents raised me to venerate my ancestors and to believe in ghosts and dragons. Why?"

Matthew approaches, saving me from having to explain. He's wearing skinny jeans with cuffs rolled to the top of his boots, and a plaid flannel shirt over a gray V-neck T-shirt. I can't help smiling, seeing him look so much like himself again.

"You look flash, Ba," I say as he sets his tray across from me and sits down. "Well, not your hair."

"I know. It's rubbish." He runs a hand through the shaggy, uneven layers. "I think the nurses cut it. The Abode has a hairdresser. I have an appointment later today."

"Nice."

I exchange glances with Lennon. Should we tell him about our dreams? Matthew takes a bite of his sandwich and munches solemnly. He has that expression I remember so well. Dreamy, far off, listening to a song only he can hear. If he had his guitar, he'd eventually start picking away at the strings before strumming the tune.

"I spoke to Helena before I came here," he finally says. "My paperwork will be ready soon. She's planning to sneak us aboard a flight to San Francisco tomorrow evening."

"Great."

"I didn't tell your mother. We can't tell anyone until we're there."

Lennon and I both nod. I have no problem with extra caution.

"There's something else I didn't tell her because I didn't want to upset her." He pauses. "I had a strange dream last night…"

My shoulders tense. No. Way.

"… about Gerry."

My mouth drops open as I gasp. Lennon and I exchange wide-eyed glances before I sputter out, "We dreamed about Gerry, too."

Matthew's brow knits tight. "Both of you?"

Lennon and I share our dreams. Matthew sits back, arms folded, head bowed, as he listens. When we're done, he looks up with troubled eyes. "It's as if he's trying to tell us something."

Is he? I assumed Gerry's ghost faded away at the end of Samhain, but maybe he lingered so he can warn us.

"When I was in a coma, I dreamed about him all the time." He pauses and a brief flash of pain squeezes his face. "Dream isn't the right word. I couldn't tell the difference between being awake and asleep. Maybe they were hallucinations. Gerry would keep me company. He'd speak, but it was like we were under water. I couldn't understand what he said. Then, last night, I dreamed he sat beside my bed, just like in hospital, only this time I could understand him."

"What did he say?" I whisper.

"He sang to me," Matthew pulls out his phone. "When he finished, I woke up. I didn't want to forget what he sang, so I recorded it." He taps the screen, and we hear his voice softly singing, though the tune has an urgent tone.

There's danger in the watchtower

> *Our love is growing bold*
> *There's danger in-between the sheets*
> *No matter how you fold*
> *There's danger in the ocean deep*
> *The water's freezing cold*
> *A dragon opens up his cave*
> *And buries you in gold.*

"A dragon." says Lennon, his eyes widening.

"He must mean Master Stoorworm," I reply. "Gerry was always telling us stories about him."

"But it was Matthew's dream, so maybe it's about Jade Dragon. Remember, the Yin Pearl gives prophetic dreams."

"But all three of us dreamed about Gerry. Could the Yin Pearl have caused that?"

"Maybe?"

Matthew's phone buzzes. His brow creases as he reads the screen. "It's from Gareth. He says, Meet me in the atrium. Bring Penny and Lennon." He slides the phone back into his pocket as he stands. "My paperwork must be done."

My chest tightens. As much as I want to return to my family, it felt good being someplace safe. Now we must expose ourselves to the world again and evade our enemies. Or fight them off. Maybe even kill again. I know Lennon feels the same way as he squeezes my hand under the table before we rise.

The station hums with activity as Beggars dressed in varying degrees of homeless despair, clutching cardboard signs scrawled with pleas for help, return from their shift in the mundane world. They situate themselves outside the institutions of power and wealth, watching who comes and goes, and report on the movement of targeted individuals with greater accuracy than CCTV. This is how the Beggar Clan earn their gelt and how they can afford to maintain an Abode like Greycoat Station. The London Beggars make the San Francisco clan look like a crew of tag-rags.

I wonder if Helena is planning to challenge Jeremiah for the leadership of the Beggar Clan and the Crossroads. That would be brilliant. Then she really would be the Beggar Queen. But would that mean giving up all hope of being with Nance?

What if Lennon decides he must be the Dragon Son after all, even if it means giving up all hope of being with me? Every step forward is a step closer to that decision. Maybe that's why I want to stay in the Abode, so we can delay the inevitable.

The atrium is the former Chadwick Street entrance to Grey-coat Station. Its arched, glass-paned roof inspired the Beggars to transform it into a secret garden. We stroll past leafy green trees spared the blight of autumn and breathe in the humid air made misty by the waterfall fountain at its center. Gareth sits on a bench amidst a bed of lavender, the purple flowers providing a bright background to his black clothes and white face.

My heart pounds. This is the exact spot where I sat with Gerry in my dream. It can't be a coincidence that we're meeting him here now.

Matthew sits beside him while Lennon and I settle cross-legged on the ground. Gareth's lips part, but then his shoulders slump and his head bows.

My heart aches. Maybe he'd started healing while we were gone, but now we're back, ripping open his wounds and reminding him of what he'd lost.

"All right?" Matthew slides an arm across his shoulders.

"No." Gareth lifts his head and takes us all in with those piercing blue eyes. "After we spoke last night, I couldn't sleep. I kept thinking about…" He spreads his hands. "Everything. I got up and went to work in our clinic, but I was rubbish. I couldn't think straight. Finally, I came here." He pats the bench. "Gerry and I used to sit here and pretend we were an ordinary couple in the park, with nobody wanting to kill us just for existing. I got sleepy, so I laid down to take a nap, and I dreamed about him."

I stifle my gasp. Neither Lennon nor Matthew say a word. The only sound is the burble of the fountain and Gareth's soft, pain-filled voice. "I was still lying here, but my head was on his lap, and he was stroking my hair."

My throat aches as I remember how much Gerry loved Gareth's soft, shiny hair.

"He said, I'm sorry. I know this is hurting you. It's hurting me, too. If I had my way, we'd never be apart. Change is coming. I'm turning the world upside-down. Wait and see.'" He turns those blue eyes to me. "Penny, are you absolutely certain he's dead?"

I can't speak because of the lump in my throat. These dreams aren't from Gerry. He would never torture us like this, especially not Gareth, with false hope. I swallow hard before answering with a whisper. "You remember what Oren Kestrel said."

Matthew stiffens. He knows that name well. "What did he say?"

I scrunch my face to keep from crying. Oren Kestrel was Gerry's oldest brother and the bane of his existence. He makes Matthew's parents look good. Hell, he makes George Lau look good. "We knew you were supposedly dead because your parents told us. We didn't know what happened to Gerry. Finally, Helena got his mother's phone number. I called and Oren Kestrel answered. He told me that Gerry had been dumped outside the London Nest. Oren took his body to a morgue, had him cremated, and spread his ashes at the crossroads."

Tears spill down my cheeks. For Strowlers, our journey's end is death. Our remains are buried in special cemeteries where our graves are lovingly tended. Spreading ashes at the crossroads is the direst of punishments, meant to doom the deceased to travel forevermore. I never allowed myself to believe that superstition, but now I must wonder. I'd hoped Gerry would find his rest after Samhain, but perhaps he never will.

Gareth kneels before me and I let go, clinging to him as I ugly cry. He kisses my cheek and strokes my hair, whispering, "It's all right. It's all right." Then his arms move to my shoulders. Hope shines from those bright blue eyes. "Maybe he lied. Maybe Gerry's not dead. Matthew's family lied about his death. Maybe Gerry's did, too."

I want to say no, that it's been too long. Gerry would've moved heaven and earth to be back with us by now if he were still alive, that Gerry's ghost visited me on Samhain, but I can't bring myself to tell him for fear of what he'd make of it. Matthew and Lennon remain silent, unwilling as I am to tell him of our dreams.

Gareth's hands slide away as he stands. He swipes his forearm across his eyes and clears his throat before he speaks. "Gerry is alive. I know it. I can feel it. There's one last thing he said. 'Don't blame the boy. Let them go.'" He takes a shaky breath. "So, I'm saying goodbye now, because I can't bear to watch you leave again. All I know is that you must win, so we can all be together again."

Matthew stands, and he and Gareth hug wordlessly. I don't watch him leave. Lennon puts his arm around me, and I weep into his shoulder.

Lennon

After Gareth leaves, Penny pulls away from my embrace and stands so she can hug Matthew. My shoulder is damp from her tears. I don't look at them. I stare into the fountain and think about what Gareth said.

Don't blame the boy.

That's twice that Dream Gerry has said he doesn't blame me. Maybe it's all wishful thinking, but I feel less awful. How weird that all four of us dreamed about him. Maybe it's Gerry's ghost, wandering the Earth after having his ashes scattered to the four winds. I shiver. Wandering ghosts are dangerous. That's why we have altars, and spirit tablets, and offerings to appease the dead. Supposedly. I stopped believing in spiritual stuff after my parents died, but now, between encounters with dragons, fairies, and maybe Gerry, I gotta wonder.

Something slithers against me, and I flinch. Not a ghost, but a more familiar presence. Jade Dragon, shrunk to the size of a seagull, perches at the top of the atrium and glares down on us.

Sup? I ask

Sup? He replies.

I smile, enjoying his confusion. *It's slang for what's up.*

I am up above you. Is that what you mean?

No. It means, like, how are you? I thought you were chilling out with the ravens at the Tower.

They showed me their treasures and spoke of many things, but I grew weary of their chatter. As he speaks, he grows larger, a heavy, oppressive presence that feels menacing. He could shatter the glass ceiling with a swish of his tail.

Why are you still here? he asks.

We gotta wait until we can go home.

Why?

Um. How do I explain paperwork to a dragon? *We need legal documents to get on an airplane.*

Nonsense. He hiss-snorts. *What about the others?*

What others?

The children. Your families.

Since when has he ever cared about them? *We're suffering and they're suffering, so that's cool with you, right? Thing is, we can't go anywhere without airplane tickets unless you're offering us another ride.*

Very well.

What? No, wait!

Dragons don't wait.

I open my mouth to warn Penny and Matthew, but before I can say a word, I'm sucked into a vortex that rushes me skyward. My body braces as I reach the roof, but I pass through without shattering the glass. London spins below me as my brain tries keeping pace with my body. Everything goes black, as if I've fainted, though I'm still conscious. I feel an undulating motion beneath me, and I realize, even before my vision clears, that I'm riding astride Jade Dragon.

Penny settles behind me and her father behind her. A translucent energy bubble holds us in place, protecting us from the elements and keeping us from squirming or trying to punch him. I can still Silent Speech yell.

You asshole! What are you doing? You can't kidnap us like this.

Except, of course, he can, and at top speed, too. London disappears in the horizon as we head for the coast.

Penny calls out, "Jade Dragon, we can't leave like this. Please. Take us back."

Why does it matter how you travel? asks the kidnapping dragon.

That's not the point. I tell him. *We didn't say goodbye to our friends.*

Are they your friends?

So, he has been paying attention. Thanks for noticing, I guess? *No.*

Then why do you care?

Because Penny and Matthew care.

Jade Dragon doesn't reply because he definitely doesn't care. He probably thinks their suffering will strengthen them.

I turn to Penny and her father. "He's not taking us back. I'm sorry. It's my fault. He wanted to know why we're still in London, and I jokingly suggested he give us another ride. I forgot dragons don't joke."

"Or ask permission," Penny adds.

"That, too."

Matthew reaches out, his fingers stroking the translucent shell of energy surrounding us. "I couldn't feel this before."

Penny and I blink in unison. She says, "Before?"

He nods, his eyes going unfocused. "I've ridden on Jade Dragon before, in my dreams, though it felt real, as if he'd used the Yin Pearl to lift my spirit from my body to show me the world."

Is that possible? I can see this asshole dragon doing it for shits and giggles, so...

"Where did he take you?" Penny asks.

"To the deepest depths of the oceans, where the strangest creatures live. Across the Himalayas to the top of Mount Everest. Dancing in a sandstorm that swept across the Saharan desert." His fingers slide away from the shell. "Everywhere but where I wanted to go, although I begged him. Just one glimpse of my family. But he never took me to see you. Never even spoke to me. I came to think of them as dream quests, a fulfillment of my longing to be free, but," He reaches out again and presses his palm to the shell. It vibrates with the flow of energy. "It was exactly like this."

None of what he says surprises me. Jade Dragon lives to explore the infinite possibilities of everything. He'd happily take Matthew for a ride just to find out how Matthew reacts and how he himself would feel about it.

Matthew pulls his phone from his pocket and stares at the screen. "It's Gareth."

Fuck. How do we explain this to Gareth and Mad Maud?

The ringing stops. Moments later, the phone pings and he reads the text.

Gareth: Where are you? Helena said you disappeared into thin air. What happened?

So, the Beggar Chief was watching us on SpyCam while we were in the atrium. No surprise, but sucky bad in terms of timing.

Matthew presses the phone to his forehead while squeezing his eyes shut.

"We can't just leave him," says Penny. "Not again. We have to say something."

This is my fault. I can't keep doing this to her, making her family suffer because of my family.

"Tell them it was me," I say with a shrug, as if I don't care. "I mean, they hate me anyway. Say something like... I don't know, like, I sneaked us out and made you promise not to tell them."

Penny shakes her head. "We won't blame you for something you didn't do."

I can see it in her stubborn face, how she's being torn between the people she loves, and I mumble, "Well, it is kinda my fault. I mean, he's kinda my dragon." Except he's not, of course. I just got stuck taking responsibility for him.

"I'll tell Gareth we don't want to involve the Beggar Clan any further in our war with George Lau." Matthew taps on his phone as he speaks. "We're sorry we left abruptly, but we didn't want Helena to stop us. We're on our way to the airport."

"We don't have our passports," Penny points out. "How do we explain that we left everything behind?"

Matthew thinks for a moment and then taps again. "Lennon's family has arranged for private transport, so we don't need our IDs."

That's almost funny. I bite my lip, so I don't laugh.

Matthew taps more without speaking, stuff between him and Gareth. Probably promising to return and bring Penny with him. Maybe that would be for the best. When she sticks around with me, weird stuff happens, like being kidnapped by dragons who don't have boundaries. I send a text to Tony.

> We've left London without being seen. I'll tell you how when I see you.

> Tell me now.

I roll my eyes. I thought I was the boss of him. As if.

> I can't. If Mad Maud contacts you, tell her you helped us escape.

As I turn off my phone, Matthew exclaims, "Damn it. Lost the signal."

I glance down and watch the coast of England disappear as we head out over the sea. I shift around, leaning against the "wall" of the bubble that holds us in place. Its energy hums through me, undulating with Jade Dragon's body as he swerves through the sky. "If this is like last time, we should be home in a few hours. Maybe we're being ungrateful. I mean, Jade Dragon is saving us a lot of hassle. Plus, our enemies won't be able to track our movement."

"True." Penny stares at the water before turning to Matthew. "Remember those times we crossed on the ferry from Liverpool to Dublin?"

He smiles. "Of course."

"Gerry would tell us stories of Master Stoorworm, who lived in the depths of the Irish Sea. How come you never told us about Jade Dragon?"

He ducks his head and takes a few moments to answer. "You know Two Dragon Clan banished me, but I never told you why. I was waiting until you were older so you'd understand. When I went to university, it was my first time away from my family and the clan, and I went a bit mad. I hung out and jammed with other musicians, smoked weed, went to raves, took Molly, and danced all night. It was amazing. The freest I ever felt in my life, but it was an illusion."

My stomach drops because I know where this is going. If there's one thing the clan won't tolerate, it's drug use. It's kind of hypocritical, because they tolerate and even encourage alcohol, but using drugs is weak and unrighteous, even if it's just weed.

"I got bold, thinking no one would notice when I went clubbing in London. I was wrong. One night, while staggering back to the tube, I got pulled into a car and taken to the *kongsi*." His mouth spreads into a thin line. "I still have the scars on my back from being disciplined. Then I was given to my parents, who took me home and yelled at me for days about how I'd disgraced them. They took me out of school and said I couldn't return until I proved I wouldn't be deviant anymore. Thing is, I was at uni for them, not me. So, I packed some clothes, grabbed my guitar, and left."

Matthew sighs before continuing. "I couldn't return to my old life, though. To be honest, I was afraid of what the clan would do to me if I did. So, I stayed clear of the clubs and played in pubs or busked in the streets, trying to earn enough to eat. Then I met your parents. Bridie caught my fancy. Caught my heart. There were rumors we all slept together, but it's always only been her, the love of my life. I gave up everything to be with her, including membership in the Two Dragon Clan. I didn't see any point in telling my children stories from a clan that rejected me. But as Kai got older, I regretted cutting him off from a part of his heritage. I'd planned to tell him everything… and then I died."

"No," says Penny, her eyes shining like emeralds, "You're alive and you have so much to tell him."

But Gerry is dead and can't tell Penny anything, except in her dreams. What more would my parents have told me, had they lived? Would the truth finally come out, or would I have lived their lies for the rest of my life?

What will I tell Tony when I get home? If I tell him that Jade Dragon gave me a ride, twice, he'll go on and on about me being the Chosen One and I'm totally not. If Dad had been honest about being Tony's father, then Tony would be the one riding on the back of a dragon. Or would he? None of this would've happened if my parents hadn't been murdered. I never would've met Penny…

Except somehow I think I would. It's weird, but regardless of anything that might've happened in the past, I feel like we've always been destined to meet. And this crazy dragon, I feel like I've always been meant to be… I dunno. His favorite pet? His almost friend? It's all fate, I guess.

Except that sucks. I mean, the meeting Penny part is awesome, but the rest is literally the worst. I'm going to have to kill my uncle. How is that even right?

Penny brushes my mind. *All right?*

Nope. How about you?

She shrugs. *I'm riding on a dragon for the second time. That's cool, I guess. I feel bad about Gareth. Being close to him again... it was like having a part of Gerry with me.*

I'm sure he felt the same about you.

Yeah. She sighs. *Is it always going to be like this? Will our families always drive a wedge between us?*

Yeah. That's not gonna change until I can get Tony to take the pearls.

Do you have to give them to him? I mean, after we're done, can't you... I dunno. Give them back to Jade Dragon instead?

Can I? I hadn't considered that before. I mean, all they've done is make my predecessors power-hungry and sleazy. The only reason the Two Dragon Clan ruled the Crossroads is because the Dragon Son used the Yang Pearl to enhance his strength during challenges. I'd be more disappointed with my dad for doing that if he hadn't already done enough to lose my respect about a thousand times over.

I'd like to believe Tony wouldn't do that, but can I be sure? He's the most honorable person I know. I'd say Auntie Cat, too, but she's lied to me, and Tony never has. And, yeah, I know. I've been a total liar to both. That's another reason I shouldn't be the Dragon Son. But since Tony won't do it, what's the point of the damn pearls, anyway?

Everyone will hate me if I give them back, I say to Penny. *But since they already do anyway, I might as well ask.*

I break contact with her and tap into Jade Dragon's consciousness. *Hey, dude. Can I ask you something?*

He doesn't reply, but he doesn't cut me off, which means he's listening.

So, your pearls, I mean, the ones you gave us. Can we, I mean, me, can I give them back?

Why would you do so?

Because they make people act really shitty.

Do they make you and your mate act shitty?

Well, no. Not yet. We killed a guy, but it was self-defense. Anyway, we're going to use the Yin and Yang Pearls to defeat my uncle and get back the Wisdom Pearl. When that's done, we were thinking maybe we should give all the pearls back to you so no one can, you know, abuse the power anymore.

Jade Dragon's tail swishes, so strong it jostles us around in the shell. Shit. Looks like I pissed him off.

What I give remains until the day has come.

What day?

He doesn't answer. Of course, he doesn't. If he did, I wouldn't have to strive and suffer. 'The day' could be tomorrow or 500 years from now. It's pointless to even wonder.

Sorry. Just thought I'd ask.

Curiosity is commendable. He breaks our connection and we're back to smooth sailing.

I connect with Penny. *He says no.*

Yeah, I kinda thought so.

I'll find a way to make Tony take the pearls.

I know you will.

Neither one of us sounds convinced.

Penny scoots around a little until her knees come to rest against my thighs. Her touch eases some of the tension from my body. I want so much for her to wrap her arms around my waist, but she can't because of her watchdog dad. It's going to be a long ride.

As Jade Dragon skims across the Atlantic Ocean, Matthew tells us more about the Yin Pearl and how he experienced what sounds like astral projection.

"It seemed so real. I can still remember it vividly, being outside the hospital, and the pearl tethering me in place." He shakes his head. "Now, I don't know if it was real or more dreams."

"Do you know anything about that?" Penny asks me.

I turn to face her. "There was a story about a Dragon Son's Wife who could float above the enemy and report on their movements, but she did it one too many times and died. Could be the same thing."

"Penny won't be attempting that," says Matthew firmly.

He doesn't see her roll her eyes, or wink at me like she totally will.

Jade Dragon gains altitude as we reach the coast of the United States. Our phones buzz again, but none of us answer. It's hard when you know your family is on the line, desperate for answers you can't give. I mean, how do you say, "I'm flying home on the back of a dragon. Don't freak out," without someone, or rather, everyone freaking out?

Also, as freaking awesome as it sounds, there's not a lot to see. It's night and Jade Dragon seems to avoid any cities. He allows me to link with him enough to know that we're flying across the southwest to avoid a snowstorm to the north. Otherwise, he's silent, intent on staying airborne with the additional burden of preserving our lives. It wasn't easy for him the first time with me and Penny, and now we have Matthew along for the ride.

Then it hits me. I cast out with the Yang Pearl before confirming my suspicion. Then I turn to Penny and her father. "We're not invisible."

They stare at me for a wide-eyed moment. "What?"

"We're taking up too much of Jade Dragon's chi. He can't maintain invisibility. His pace has slowed, too."

"Can he carry us the entire way?" asks Matthew.

Fair question. If he can't and has to drop us off somewhere, we'll be screwed.

"Has he asked for help?" asks Penny.

Of course, he hasn't. He wants us to figure it out like good little hatchlings. What could we do to help? The answer glows against my chest.

I turn to Penny and hold up my hand. Her palm presses against mine, her cool touch sending heat and energy through me. I send the same through her until the Yin and the Yang Pearls combine and become one. We breathe in unison as our mingled *chi* flows toward the great pearl embedded in Jade Dragon's chest. Within lies all the wisdom and knowledge of Jade Dragon and his ancestors, going back to prehistoric times... no, farther back, to when humans were still monkeys.

Dragons, all that they are, all their memories, pass genetically to their spawn and stored in their pearls. Jade Dragon gave us these pearls as his offspring. Giving them back would be a slap in the snout and insulting his ancestors.

Sorry, dude.

Jade Dragon doesn't answer but continues accepting our *chi* as an apology. We become invisible again and pick up speed gliding across Texas. He also blocks any further attempt to delve into his pearl. I want to follow that source of energy and swim in the knowledge of the ages. Why won't he let me?

He wants us to get our own knowledge, remember? says Penny.

Yeah, but he's got all that ancestral knowledge, so it doesn't seem fair.

Maybe he had to earn it.

Yeah. And suffer for it.

Still, I know this dragon. He's hiding something. I can't let frustration overcome the steady flow of my chi, so I release it and ride the dragon as one with Penny.

Invisible, we travel through another dimension. Earth, not Earth. Time changes, shortens, lengthens, as we wind through the strands, both here and there, guided by our pearl. I'm me, not me, moving through seconds and centuries, existing in all moments and in none.

A tingling sensation moves through me and I'm here, me, just me, no longer one with Jade Dragon and Penny. I exhale as the ache of euphoria drains from my body. I peer through the bubble. San Francisco glitters below us as if suspended in time, awaiting our arrival.

That. Was a trip.

Penny squeezes my hand. Her dazed expression matches how I feel.

"Are you okay?" I ask.

She nods. "So that's how he travels. Did you know?"

I scoff. "Of course not."

She turns to Matthew. "Are you all right, Ba? I'm sorry we had to phase out like that."

"I'm fine." He stares at us with troubled eyes. Not angry exactly, but I think if he could shove me off Jade Dragon so I'd leave Penny alone, he would. Rather than deal with that, I connect with Jade Dragon.

Hey, don't drop us off in the park again, okay?

Why would I do that?

Is there any point in reminding him that's exactly what he did in London?

I will leave you in the place of greatest safety.

Yeah, like I trust that isn't the middle of the Chinatown police station or some other random location. *How about the roof of the kongsi?*

Not inside?

I look at the time on my phone. It's after midnight. I don't want to scare the shit out of our families. Then again, Uncle George's spies won't see us arrive if we're inside.

Inside is good, but not in front of anyone, okay?

Very well.

Thanks. I gotta dig deep because I'm still pissed off at his kidnapping ass. *And thanks for giving us a ride home. I know you meant well, but next time, ask people before you grab them and take them some place.*

If I asked, you would talk and weigh options, and surrender to your fears.

He's not wrong, but that's not the point. I finish that thought and the next thing I know, I'm sitting on a carpeted floor in a dark room with Penny and Matthew beside me. I squeeze my eyes shut against the feeling like I've been in an elevator that descended too rapidly. Then I take out my phone and turn on the flashlight, and I know exactly where we are: the nursery.

I stand and shake my legs to get the blood flowing before lurching over to turn on the light switch next to the door. It's a little funny seeing Penny and Matthew blinking around at our unlikely location. I haven't been in the room since I painted the wall with pink dolphins frolicking in the ocean. The paint has since dried and now it's all set up with a crib, a rocking chair, a twin bed, all that new baby stuff.

"Where are we?" whispers Matthew as he stands.

"The San Francisco *kongsi*," I reply in a hushed tone. "Actually, the second floor, where my brother lives. He and his wife are going to have a baby."

Penny examines the ocean scene. "The photos don't do this justice. It looks amazing."

"Thanks." It feels good to get some praise for my work. I mean, May said nice things, but Tony just stared and nodded, like I'd painted the wall a solid color.

"You painted that?" asks Matthew.

"Yeah." I'd asked May what I could do for the baby, and this is what she wanted, pink dolphins. They're an endangered species in Hong Kong and she's into conservation.

He frowns and squints, as if I've stepped out of a box and now he has to figure me out all over again. That's his problem.

"What should we do?" asks Penny.

Good question. What can we do that won't startle the shit out of our families? The answer: nothing. I take out my phone and text Tony.

Don't freak out. We're in the nursery.

What do you mean, the nursery?

Here. Your baby's nursery.

We don't hear anything because you won't hear Tony coming. Moments later, the door swings open and he enters the room. He freezes before blinking once. Then he whispers the words I dread.

"Jade Dragon."

Penny

Lennon's shoulders lift in a tight shrug. "Um, yeah."

Tony keeps staring at us like we're ghosts, until I finally say, "Tony, this is my father, Matthew."

He gives Matthew a wary nod before saying, "You were in a coma, and they used the pearls to heal you."

"Yes." Matthew's mouth twists, as if he's keeping himself from adding, 'obviously.'

That Tony doesn't smile or offer congratulations isn't surprising, but I think it's something more. Matthew is proof that Lennon and I used the pearls together successfully, and he doesn't like it.

"It doesn't matter how we got here," says Lennon. "We're here and Uncle George doesn't know, which is a huge advantage, right?"

That snaps Tony out of it. "Dragon Son, come with me." He glances at me and Matthew. "Wait here while we tell your family. Stay away from the windows. We're being spied on by drones."

Lennon and I exchange looks as he heads out the door behind Tony. We're being divided again, his family and mine, and they'll be even more determined than Gareth and Helena to keep us apart.

A few minutes later, I hear startled exclamations and the pounding of feet in the hallway. Matthew takes my hand. I squeeze tight as my mother and brother rush into the room.

It's hard to describe Bridie's face. Pure joy, yes, but more than that. There's a hesitancy when she sees him. A painful catch in her gasp. Deep sorrow etched in her features and something more. Shame.

That's the Wongs doing. They made her ashamed of her actions, even though they're the ones who gulled her into marrying Bill and moving to SF.

Matthew's face mirrors the same joy and sorrow. He and Gerry went on the dub and didn't return. Where she has shame, he has guilt. His parents' treachery destroyed our family.

Kai has no baggage. He runs into his father's arms, laughing and crying, and repeating over and over again, "Ba, Ba!"

Matthew holds his son close, strokes the back of his head and kisses his cheeks before holding him at arm's length. Tears roll down his cheeks as he chokes out, "You're not a child anymore."

Bridie covers her mouth to muffle her sobs. Matthew lets go of Kai and turns to her with open arms. She goes to him, and they embrace, so fully. They meld together as if one person, crying one set of tears. Their bodies shake and quiver as they share sloppy kisses all over each other's faces.

Then they part and hold up their arms for Kai to join them. He enters their embrace, and they are complete. Mother, father, son. A family reunited.

I smile, though my soul hurts from the stabbing in my heart. They are a complete family, and I am not. I never will be, not without Gerry. He'll always be that lost part of me.

Then Bridie and Matthew part again and open their arms, gesturing for me to join them. I don't hesitate. I'm drawn into their embrace, feel the reassurance of their arms around me, smell their sweat, am drenched in their tears, and I allow myself to feel almost whole.

Finally, we part. Bridie looks at me and Matthew, shaking her head as she says, "But how did you get here so quickly? It's only been a few hours since Helena called to tell us you'd disappeared. There aren't any planes that fly so fast, are there?"

Matthew and I exchange glances. What to say? It wouldn't be hard to sham her. She never pays attention to the news or anything technical beyond her immediate needs. Kai, on the other hand, will be on his phone in a hot second, googling types of airplanes. Besides, I'm done being fake.

I settle on the rocking chair and gesture for everyone to take a seat. Bridie and Kai sit on the bed with Matthew between them, her clinging to his arm as if afraid he'll float away.

How to say it? Just say it, I guess. "Jade Dragon brought us back."

Bridie blinks before laughing. She starts to speak, but words fade from her lips as she gazes from me to Matthew and sees no joke.

Kai's mouth drops open before he says, "No. Way. For real?"

I nod.

"Holy shit!"

Mum shakes her head. "He'll want something in return. Eldritch beings always do."

I don't point out we're already deep in Jade Dragon's debt for using his pearls to heal Matthew. "He didn't say anything about it."

"Dragons aren't fairies. It's doubtless implied."

"I think when he does things, it's because he wants them to happen. For whatever reason, he wants us here. I don't know why." I squirm, unable to ignore my needs after being on a dragon for hours. Then I stand. "Sorry, but I need to use the bathroom."

Bridie and Kai give me blank stares, as if they forgot I was human and have a bladder. As I leave the room, they turn to Matthew, who starts telling them of his dealings with Jade Dragon.

I've been on this floor a few times and know where to find the bathroom. It's weird because when I was here as Aaron's best friend's sister, I was gold. Offered cookies and tea and sat down for friendly chats with May. Tony doesn't do friendly, but he made it clear I was welcome within the boundaries of that role. After they discovered my relationship with Lennon, they yanked the welcome mat out from under me. I doubt they have any enthusiasm for my presence in their home right now, but oh well.

After seeing to my needs, I gulp down several handfuls of water until I feel less thirsty. I wish I could go to the kitchen and get a glass, but that might interrupt Lennon and his family. When I return to the nursery, Matthew stands.

"Third door on the left," I tell him sympathetically.

I settle back in the rocking chair and face my wide-eyed mother and brother. I begin with Halloween night, when I'd fled the Nest to rendezvous with Lennon, and how Jade Dragon decided to give us a ride. When Matthew returns, we share the story of our flight home. We're about finished when there's a tap on the door.

Aaron stands in the doorway, staring at us tongue-tied, as if he'd forgotten what he was going to say.

Kai jumps to his feet. "Dude, come in. Meet my dad. Ba, this is Aaron, Tony's younger brother. Aaron, this is my dad, Matthew."

Matthew stands as well and smiles warmly, holding out his hand as if he didn't know Aaron's father was one of the men responsible for his near-death.

Aaron, looking as though he's very aware, ducks his head as they shake. "Hi. Um, Tony wants you guys to come into the living room, okay?"

Tony, not Lennon. As if there's any doubt who's in charge.

This is confirmed when we enter the living room. Tony sits enthroned in the single, regal armchair while Lennon perches on the ottoman. Why can't he just be the bloody Dragon Son and do us all a favor?

After awkward introductions, Bridie and Matthew join May on the couch. Aaron plops on the floor and Kai settles cross-legged beside him. That's good to see. I'd hate for all this conflict to ruin their friendship. I join Lennon on the ottoman while Cat and Roy settle on the love seat. Their knees touch and fingers brush, but they don't hold hands, though I can tell they want to. I'd think of them as couple goals, except they let clan conflict keep them apart for 20 years. Should I be so judge-y? The same thing could happen to me and Lennon.

I sigh, wishing I could lean against Lennon, rest my head on his shoulder and close my eyes. We're the most powerful people in the room, but we live under the judgment of our relatives.

Tony looks at Lennon as he speaks. "Will Jade Dragon aid us further against our enemies?"

Lennon exchanges glances with me before shrugging. "Maybe? I mean, probably not. He's left me hanging a lot."

"What's Jade Dragon like?" asks Aaron.

"He's like… a dragon." Lennon turns to me as if hoping I'll have a better description. I don't.

"He's old, and yet young, almost childlike," answers Matthew, his eyes faraway and dreamy. "As powerful as a storm raging across a desert, and wiser than any sage. He will spend an infinite amount of time on the smallest imaginable thing so he can fully comprehend it. He's not human and doesn't share our feelings, yet he was once human, so he understands those feelings. Dragons can't love us, but they can care about an outcome. I believe Jade Dragon cares about ours."

"Will he help us?" asks Tony.

"Yes, but as he will, not as we want."

Lennon nods. "He's got that right."

A heavy silence falls over the room. Then Kai asks, "What about Master Stoorworm? Is he real?"

"He's real," I reply. "I've had…" I search for the right word, "encounters with him."

"What kind of encounters?"

"The dragon kind. Mostly dreams."

Bridie shakes her head, her eyes troubled. "These dragons sound like fairies, and fairies always want something for their labor. They want something from us."

"Jade Dragon wants us to succeed," says Tony. "He founded our clan and created our martial arts so that we could be the most powerful of those who walk the Crossroads."

"Master Stoorworm did the opposite. Abandoned his offspring to be outcasts and wanderers." She lifts her chin. "But we're the stronger for it."

"No," Lennon says abruptly. I can feel the tension in his body as his hands squeeze the edge of the ottoman. "You're both wrong. These dragons, they do what they do because they want to see what will happen. Jade Dragon told me our clan ignored his guidance and made our own rules, and he let us because it was interesting to watch. Like, that whole 'Dragon Son should be the first-born son of the first-born son' deal. That's a human thing. He doesn't care about that. He doesn't even care if the Dragon Son is male or female. It could be any of his descendents, even May or Kai."

Tony stands, glaring down on Lennon. His words come out like bullets. "Dragon Son. Come with me. Now."

Lennon doesn't cower. He meets his brother's gaze and nods. Tony turns and heads out of the room without a backwards glance.

I feel Lennon's sigh as he reaches out to me. *I guess I pissed him off.*

My eyebrows raise. *You think?*

Lol. See you later. He rises to follow Tony.

Don't let him bully you. I call after him.

He doesn't bully. He dominates. It's different.

And Lennon doesn't do either. Maybe that's why I love him. I look at my mother, hand in hand with Matthew, her cheek resting on his shoulder. Maybe that's why she fell in love with him, and Gerry, too. Maybe the Wayward Way was created for people who can't stomach the bullying and domination allowed by the strict moral code of the Glory Road.

May turns to the rest of us, one hand caressing her swollen belly as if soothing the restless child within. "The bedrooms are being arranged so that no one sleeps alone, for safety's sake. Kai has already been staying with Aaron. Bridie, Matthew will be in your room, of course. Penny, you'll share with Auntie Cat, and Lennon will stay with Uncle Roy."

I can't help squinting. Is it really for safety's sake, or an elaborate way of making sure Lennon and I don't wind up in each other's beds? I feel bad for putting Cat and Roy out, but then again, since they're not married, chances are they aren't allowed to sleep together.

I shift so I'm sitting in the warmth Lennon left behind. Why can't Tony give him a break? Doesn't he realize how tired we are? A sudden sense of fatigue weighs me down. All I want right now is a hot shower and a good night's sleep in my own bed...

Huh. I'm forgetting how to be a Strowler. I've gotten

attached to having my own room. My shoulders sag as I think of my business, Pinafores and More, and all the orders I had to cancel. Will I ever get those customers back? Do I even want to? Or do I want to spend my days singing and dancing with my family while we travel the world?

And what about Lennon?

My eyes close against the ache forming in my head and I feel the warm glow of the Yin Pearl against my skin. I need to set aside the what-ifs and save my energy for what lies ahead. My family has no future if we don't defeat George Lau.

Lennon

As we enter the dining room, I already know what we're going to say, like words in a play. Our own personal tragedy. Tony heads for his spot at the head of the table before stopping abruptly. I can see the wheels in his head turn. If I'm the Dragon Son, then I'm the head of the family, not him, and the place of honor belongs to me. Expressionless, he steps aside, gesturing me toward the Patriarchal Throne.

I roll my eyes because, God, why? Can't we just sit like people? I walk around the Penultimate Glory and take an ordinary chair with no bullshit attached. Big Brother's eyes squeeze tight before he sits across from me. I fold my hands on the tabletop and wait because, despite all this crap, we both know who's in charge.

"You must not share Jade Dragon's secrets with outsiders," he begins.

"Jade Dragon doesn't have secrets. Don't you get it?" I huff because I can tell from his pinched lips he doesn't. "You know when Dad would talk to Jade Dragon at the Summoning Ceremony? That was all bullshit. Jade Dragon told me Dad never spoke to him, that they couldn't make the connection because he was too full of guilt. So, that stuff he claimed Jade Dragon said? Lies."

Tony sits back, his clenched hands sliding into his lap. I should stop, but he needs to understand. "Jade Dragon watches us like we're his favorite TV show. He doesn't have some big moral agenda for us. He doesn't care about our sex, or birth order, or our parents, or anything like that, unless it makes watching us more interesting. And even then, if we get too predictable, he gets bored and flies away."

"If that's true, then why did he help you? Not just once, but many times."

"And a lot of times he didn't help me. I begged him to give me the Yin Pearl so I could save John Walks Long. He refused. He said we lost it, so we had to find it, even though he knew the whole time Matthew had it. Just like he knew your dad… I mean, Uncle George had the Wisdom Pearl and didn't tell us."

Tony looks at me like I'm a priest who won't give him the answer he needs; that his suffering isn't pointless, that his god isn't playing with him and discarding him like a broken toy. There is something I can say that might help.

"Jade Dragon told me we can only gain wisdom through striving and suffering. If we die, or someone we love dies, then it was in pursuit of wisdom, so it was worth it. I don't know why he chooses when he helps me, but I think it has something to do with that."

Tony's dull eyes brighten. He nods along as I speak. "Of course. He's a dragon. We shouldn't question his ways."

Shouldn't we? I decide not to add that Jade Dragon can be a dick. It won't help. Besides, Big Brother is of the suffer-to-wisdom model, and he can be a dick, too. This Dragon Son shit is so wasted on me, but he refuses to see it. Check it out.

"How are things here?" I ask.

"Things are as you left them. We can do nothing without the guidance of the Dragon Son."

And we're off.

My turn. "I've been gone for almost a week and you haven't done anything?"

There's a pinch between his eyebrows before he launches into a long list of all he's done to secure our *kongsi* and strengthen the support of our allies.

When he finishes, I say, "Great. Thanks." The pinch deepens. Both he and Dad would've responded to the report of a subordinate with a single manly nod, but that kind of masculinity didn't swim its way through the gene pool to me. Another reason I'm a shitty Dragon Son. I'm way too chill for this job. All I can think to say next is, "So, what's the deal with Uncle George?"

"You mean, the Traitor?"

He can't refer to his former father as his uncle, or even speak his name. That's another way he and I are wired differently. My relationships with other people are an ongoing thing, depending on our latest interaction. Tony puts people in a box, shuts the lid, and labels it. That label defines his relationship with you. For example, he's trying to change my label from "Little Brother" to "Dragon Son," but I won't let him and it's pissing him off. He's changed Uncle George's label from "Father" to "Traitor" with nothing in-between. He'll never accept him as "Uncle" and I can't blame him for that.

"Yeah, him. He seems to be a lot more powerful than when he was here, and that was only two weeks ago. Does anyone know what happened?"

I feel Tony's consciousness brush against mine, and I let him in.

The compound is now under complete control of the Traitor. Anyone loyal to you either fled or is now enthralled with one exception, a deaf woman named Kwan-Yi. Her parents are the priests who keep our ancestral hall. She can't speak, but she can read lips. What

I'm about to say comes from her. To maintain her safety, we cannot speak of her aloud.

I nod solemnly. *How's she been able to communicate with you?*

The Traitor is monitoring all cell phone signals coming out of the compound. However, Kwan-Yi attends an online school for the deaf. She's been sending me messages through that account, despite the danger. Tony bows his head for a moment in respect for her courage.

The Traitor has had only limited use of the Wisdom Pearl. Apparently, Head Elder was too strong for the Traitor to have any sway over him. He wanted to know why, so when they returned to the clan compound, he summoned Fifth Elder to meet him at the Altar of the Elders. Kwan-Yi was working in an adjacent chamber and saw everything.

My stomach twists. Fifth Elder is Head Elder's oldest son. I call him Uncle Tool because that's what he is to his father. I hate them and blame them for the deaths of my parents, but will this be the revenge I sought?

The Traitor used the Wisdom Pearl to persuade Fifth Elder to tell him Head Elder's secret. As you know, during the Taiping Rebellion, our clan lost the manuals describing how to use the dragon pearls. Fifth Elder revealed that the Wisdom Pearl's manual was recovered shortly after the rebellion.

My mouth drops open and I say, "What?" aloud.

Tony nods grimly. *The Head Elders since then have kept the manual hidden from everyone, including the Dragon Son. Every Head Elder has read that manual to learn how to use the Wisdom Pearl if it's found, or resist it if it falls into the wrong hands. Since Fifth Elder was to be the next Head Elder, he knew this secret, though he hadn't read the manual. He even knew its hiding place, in a secret compartment within the Altar of the Elders, and he retrieved the manual for the Traitor.*

Once the Traitor had it in hand, he summoned Head Elder to join them. Then he had them enter the caverns with him. Kwan-Yi was too afraid to move for fear of revealing herself, so she stayed where she was. About an hour later, the Traitor returned without Head Elder and his son. He went to Jade Dragon's altar and removed the Summoning Pearl from the spirit tablet.

What? I manage not to say that aloud, though I'm equally shocked. *How did he get away with all that?*

Head Elder. Before leaving for San Francisco, he fortified the compound with those loyal to the Traitor.

I shake my head. *I don't get it. What was in it for him?*

Your cousin, Wai-Lam.

I have to think for a moment, because I always called her by her English name. *You mean, Claire? What about her?* Even as I ask that, I know I'm going to hate the answer. Claire is Fifth Elder's daughter. She's a year older than me.

They made a deal. The Traitor would declare Aaron a bastard, marry Wai-Lam, and their son would be the future Dragon Son.

My grandfather is conniving as hell. I'm sure he planned to get rid of Uncle George, the same way he got rid of my dad, as soon as a new, easily manipulated heir was born. As if Uncle George couldn't figure that out. *So, I guess Head Elder and Fifth Elder are dead.*

No one has seen them since that day.

Stabbed in the back, just like they deserved. I guess that's revenge, except it's Uncle George who got it, not me. I should be angry or happy, or something, but I feel numb. And a little relieved it wasn't me who killed my mother's father and brother.

I sigh aloud. *Well, at least Claire is off the hook.*

The Traitor married her last summer.

What? Why didn't we hear about it?

It was done in secret at the Wanchai kongsi. According to Kwan-Yi, she's at the compound now and she's pregnant.

That is so disgusting. I don't know Claire very well, mostly because I hate her dad, but I had nothing against her. Head

Elder used her the way he tried using me, only worse. We're not grandchildren. We're pawns. *Why is the Traitor still alive? Isn't anyone doing anything to stop him?*

Second Elder hired Shinobi to assassinate him.

I wince as if he'd gut-punched me. Shinobi killed my… our father. Not to mention the fact that Hasaki, head Shinobi of the local Kasumi Clan, killed John Walks Long. Then I remember something Hasaki said to me: *Do you blame the weapon or the one who fired the weapon?* On the Crossroads, it's forbidden to retaliate against assassins. It'd be like retaliating against a gun or a knife. It's up to the injured party to discover who hired that weapon and retaliate against them. So why not use that same weapon to take revenge?

Cool. How's that going?

I spoke to Second Elder earlier today. She told me that several Shinobi had infiltrated the compound last night. Their bodies were left outside the gate this morning.

Well, shit. Not a huge surprise, though. I mean, people hire the Two Dragon Clan to protect them from assassins. The only way they could kill Dad is because Uncle George took part in the ambush. I rub my forehead. *Okay, then. Penny and I have the pearls. I guess we go to the compound and take him on.*

You and Penny?

You have someone else in mind?

We stare at each other across the desk.

How will you and Penny enter the compound?

We'll need help. Maybe someone can cause a distraction. I'll bet Brother Ash would do it.

Tony frowns at the name of Hong Kong's Beggar Chief. *We cannot put ourselves any further in debt to the Beggar Clan. We need you in a position to challenge Jeremiah.*

Yeah. About that. I suck in air between my teeth before I tell him about the deal I made with Mad Maude.

Tony doesn't blink, which means on the inside, he's exploding. I can tell because he cuts contact with me to speak aloud. "One hundred years."

"Yeah." I manage not to squirm.

"No. She coerced you. We don't honor that."

"She totally coerced me, but we do have to honor it because I'm not a kid anymore. Isn't that how the Crossroads works?"

You shouldn't have given in to her demands. Tony switches back to Silent Speech, though I wish he wouldn't since my *chi* is worn thin.

I had to pay my debt, and I had nothing else to give.

Tony leans back and gives me that thousand-mile stare. *When the clan learns of this, many will defect to the Traitor's side.*

I'm so sick of having to abide by everyone else's bullshit. It gives me a head full of steam and I blow it off by shouting, "Good! Let them. Who needs them, anyway? If that's all it takes for them to betray us, then they can fuck off. Our clan is better off without them. The Two Dragon Clan isn't what it used to be, and you know it. I mean, we were once these badass martial artists who protected people, but now we're like, I don't know, a corporation or something. Why do you think I let Jeremiah Walks Long win our challenge? Because we suck. The Beggar Clan is way more righteous than us. I want the Two Dragon Clan to go back to its roots and whoever doesn't like it can leave, defect, whatever, I don't care. I'm the Dragon Son and that's my decision, so that's how it's gonna be."

There's a long silence. Then Tony nods. *You're right. We have lost our way. Our father and the Traitor, they embody that loss. We must root out all the corruption and make the clan what it once was.* He rubs his chin as his eyes become unfocused. *Dedicated, disciplined martial artists who serve honor and righteousness instead of wealth and fame. That must be why Jade Dragon allowed so much evil to flourish, to teach us the perils of greed and force us to return to what we once were.*

I nod along because, sure, why not? He won't listen if I tell him differently.

How long will Mad Maud keep this secret?

Until we defeat Uncle Traitor.

Good. We can't afford any more defections.

There've been defections?

Tony gives a single, grim nod. *The Traitor has used his power of persuasion to draw local clan members to him.*

Are they staying in the city or going to join him in Hong Kong?

They're going to the Eighty-Eight.

The Eighty-Eight? You mean, that new building downtown? The one with the dragon gate?

Another grim nod.

Why there?

Because the Two Dragon Clan owns the floor above the dragon gate.

What? Are you kidding me? I don't even want to think of how many millions of dollars that must've cost.

You didn't know?

No. No one tells me anything. You know that.

I know you left your home in anger and when you returned, you took no interest in clan affairs.

That's not fair. The Eighty-Eight has been under construction for years. Dad never said anything to me about it. I don't get it. Why would he want an entire floor in some dumb skyscraper?

Head Elder made the purchase. He considers our kongsi to be an unworthy home for the Dragon Son and the Two Dragon Clan. That floor was to be the new San Francisco kongsi.

My mouth drops open. *No way. I can't imagine Dad agreeing to that.*

He didn't. It was one of the many bones of contention between him and Head Elder. However, I don't believe Head Elder ever intended for our father to live there. He had it built for you to be the home of the new dragon.

I snort. Like I'd ever agree to live in the Financial District, which is, like, the most uncool part of the city, among a bunch of rich, asshole techies.

Tony continues, *Our grandmother's family provided the finances. As you know, they always preferred the Traitor. I believe they've been planning this for years, to overthrow our father, bypass you, and make him the Dragon Son. The Eighty-Eight was ultimately intended to be his home.*

Now, that makes sense. Uncle George would definitely want to live there, above a dragon gate in a building numbered 88. For a moment, I almost feel bad for Auntie Sylvia. If she'd stuck with him, she'd have eventually got what she wanted. She hated the *kongsi* and constantly complained about living in a ghetto. She'd have loved the Eighty-Eight. Living there would've made her feel like a queen. How fucking sad is that? I guess that's karma for being a murderer.

Tony's eyes tighten without blinking. *My mother never would've lived there. The Traitor never forgave her for giving birth to me.*

Oh. Shit. I broadcasted that. *Big Brother, I'm sorry. I…*

You're tired. Go to bed. He gets up and leaves without a glance back at me.

I flop back in my chair and rub my forehead. I'm the worst secret brother in the world. Plus, I understand how he feels now. Penny can tell me a thousand times that she doesn't blame me for the death of her father, but do I believe her? No. Then again, I really don't blame Tony for his mother's actions at all. Maybe I should believe Penny, but I can't, any more than Tony believes me.

I sigh out a long groan. I don't want to think about it anymore. All I want to do is sleep. I'm ready to flop anywhere. The couch will be fine, since I'm sure Big Brother doesn't want to deal with me anymore tonight.

As if on cue, the kitchen door swings open. Tony holds out

a pair of pajama bottoms and a T-shirt. After I take them, he jerks his head to follow him. We head down the hall without speaking. Light shines through the bottom cracks of the doors we pass. In some ways, the *kongsi* is like a small hotel. The top three floors each have ten bedrooms, meant to house family, staff, and a constant flow of visitors. The visits stopped after my parents died. As far as I know, no one has stayed on the top floor since then. My grandfather died up there, and my mother, too. Maybe no one will ever stay there again. It feels cursed.

Tony stops in front of a door, knocks twice, and strides away. The door opens and Uncle Roy steps aside, revealing one of the larger guest rooms, with two beds.

"I'm staying with you?" I ask.

He nods.

"Why don't I have my own room?"

"We're all doubled up for safety. Penny is staying with Cat."

I guess that works as an excuse to keep the unmarried people away from each other. I'm too tired to complain. Luckily, this room has its own bathroom. I take a shower to wash away the faint, reptilian scent of Jade Dragon that lingers on my skin and hair. Hopefully, I can borrow more clothes from Tony in the morning if he's not too ticked off with me.

Roy is sitting up in bed, texting, but slips the phone under the duvet as I reenter the room. It's kinda cute, the way he and Auntie Cat still act like guilty teens. He eyes me in that grave way of his. "There's something I want to say that you probably don't want to hear…"

Probably not, but that won't stop him.

"Your father would be very proud of you."

It's weird how that hits me in the gut. I don't care how Dad would've felt about anything I've done, or at least that's what I tell myself. He's a fucking hypocrite who would've reamed me for my relationship with Penny. I hate him. So why do I still want him to be proud of me? How messed up is that?

I shrug like Dad means nothing to me and climb into bed. My phone buzzes. It's Penny.

I have my phone back. Bridie got it from Uncle Christy before she left the Nest.

Roy's phone buzzes, too. We look at each other. He nods. I nod back, and he turns off the light. Then we both roll over so we can message our girlfriends in private.

You ok?

Yeah. I'm with Cat.

I'm with Roy.

Lucky us. Lucky them.

I smile. She always makes me feel better about a shitty situation.

You ok?

I'm tired. Tell you about it tomorrow.

Ok. Night 🩶

Night 🩶

Yeah. Much better.

I close my eyes and feel an undulating motion beneath me, as if I'm still riding Jade Dragon. It's like trying to fall asleep after being on a rollercoaster. After a while, the sensation fades, and I drift off...

Jade Dragon swoops between the towers of the Golden Gate Bridge, causing gusts strong enough to knock over pedestrians on the walkway. He's such an asshole!

"Cut it out," I yell.

He ignores me, of course, and dives into the bay. I hold my breath until I realize the protective bubble is keeping me dry and allowing me to breathe. Why is he doing this? Stupid question. Why does he do anything? He undulates as we move through the murky depths…

… rolling and shifting in a violent motion as if swimming against a storm. My eyes pop open. I'm not on Jade Dragon, but my bed is swaying back and forth.

The light goes on as Uncle Roy shouts, "Earthquake!"

Penny

Cat all but shoves me under the desk before anchoring herself in the bathroom doorway. The building tilts and sways, gaining speed to become a proper shake before slowing to a groaning to a halt. I press my hand to my heart and breathe.

"Are you all right?" asks Cat, still bracing herself as I crawl out from my cramped shelter.

"I'm fine. You?"

She nods before hurrying out the bedroom door. I glance at the clock on the nightstand. It's 7:27 a.m. Ugh! Couldn't it wait until later in the morning so I could get more sleep? Natural disasters are like Jade Dragon. They just happen.

I follow Cat into the hallway, where everyone except Bridie and Matthew are milling about, questioning each other. I'm about to go to their room when the building shakes again.

"Aftershock," Aaron calls out.

Everyone dashes under a doorframe, but the shaking stops within seconds. We wait before collectively exhaling.

Tony makes the first move, striding down the hallway, phone pressed to his ear. Lennon, Aaron, May, Cat, and Roy follow him, but stop as he comes to an abrupt halt. He turns to

Lennon. "Stay here. Your presence in the *kongsi* must remain secret."

I go to Lennon's side as his family moves back into action.

"But I'm the Dragon Son," he mutters.

I pat his arm. "Sure ya are."

Kai knocks on a closed door. "Mum, Ba, are you okay?"

"Just a moment," Bridie's muffled voice calls out.

"They must be getting dressed," I say. "I'm going to do the same."

"Me, too," replies Kai, heading back to his room.

Lennon looks from him to me, puzzled. "Why aren't you guys more scared?"

"What do you mean?" I ask. "I am scared."

"You seem kinda calm for your first earthquake."

"Oh." I shake my head. "No. This isn't our first one. We traveled through Italy one summer, performing at the Irish pubs, and a big earthquake hit while we were staying in Perugia, way bigger than this one. That was terrifying."

He squints. "There are a lot of Irish pubs in Italy?"

"There are Irish pubs everywhere. You'd be surprised. In Amsterdam, we'd have a gig in a different pub every night." I smile, thinking back on that, playing in canal-side pubs and having a blast, despite getting eaten alive by mosquitoes.

Lennon gets that look on his face, that wistful gaze that says he thinks he's losing me, and he's going to let me go so I can be happy. As if I can be truly happy without him.

After everyone gets dressed, we head for the kitchen, but have to hold back on hunger. Broken dishes litter the floor and counters, splattered and soaked with the oozing contents of shattered bottles. Cookware is scattered across the kitchen and cans have rolled across the debris to settle where they will. Nothing can be done but clean, so that's what we do.

Lennon manages to find the remote and turns on the TV

bolted into the cabinet next to the sink. Across the screen, a banner reads, "5.7 Earthquake Rocks the Bay Area."

Kai scoffs. "It was 6.6 in Perugia."

Moments later, as if in response, the building rattles. It lasts only a few seconds. Not long enough for us to react beyond bracing ourselves.

"I hope there aren't many more of those," says Bridie. "They went on for days in Perugia…" Her voice trails off as she pulls a vibrating phone from her sweater pocket. She stares at the screen, rolls her eyes, and shoves it back in.

"Who's that?" I ask.

"Christy."

No way. The utter nerve of him. "What does he want?"

"He wants me to call him."

"Are you going to?"

"No. He can bugger off."

"Too right, Mum," declares Kai.

Matthew nods. "We need to stay away from our families. They've caused us enough harm."

Bridie snaps, "Oh, bugger," and snatches the phone from her pocket again to scowl at the screen.

"Why don't you turn it off?" I ask.

"I can't. I'm still the property manager at our building."

"Do you have to go there?"

"No." She chews her lip before glancing apologetically at Matthew. "The owners think we're back in London. I told them Charles died, and we had to return to attend his funeral."

He shrugs. "He's dead to me."

"Same with Christy," declares Bridie, though with less conviction. "Anyway, the owners have been messaging me and I have to reply. I left my work phone in the building, but they have my personal number, so…" She sighs. "Once this unpleasantness is over, I'll quit, and we'll move back to London…"

"… where we'll buy a caravan and go back to traveling," Matthew finishes.

The smile they share warms my heart. There's so much going against us, but we have to win so they can live in peace and get back some of what they'd lost.

After we're done cleaning, Bridie says, "Right, then, how about some oatmeal?"

"Are there sausages?" I ask hopefully.

She smiles. "Yes. May was kind enough to order groceries for us yesterday. Plenty of everything. I'll make enough for everyone."

"I'll help."

"Me, too," says Kai.

We get to work, Bridie stirring the oats, while I chop the dried fruit, and Kai gets the sausages sizzling. I listen to the news while we work. In Oakland, a huge container crane collapsed, shutting down the entire port for inspection. In SF, the Titanic is the big story. No, not the ship, but an equally doomed skyscraper. Its actual name is the Titanium Tower, which started sinking into the landfill almost as soon as they built it. It's occasionally on the news, with its tenants and owners threatening to sue each other and contractors promising to find a solution. Looks like there was no solution because the damn thing is actually tilting now. Residents are being interviewed on the street, unable to enter their condos with the billion-dollar views. Bleaters dump their money into the stupidest things.

The news shifts to the 88, a skyscraper still under construction in close vicinity to the Titanic. It's famous for two reasons: its Chinese investors paid a fortune for that address with its lucky double eight address, and it's the first building in San Francisco with a dragon gate. A helicopter camera zooms in on the square hole constructed in the top third of the building, searching for any potential damage. It's too small for a dragon to fly through. Then again, Jade Dragon can shrink in size. I wonder if he already has. It seems like the sort of thing he'd like to do. Travel the world and fly through all the dragon gates until he got bored and found something else to capture his attention. Like an earthquake. I sense his presence and can tell he's one happy boy.

"Construction will be halted on the 88 until inspectors can ascertain if any damage was done to the structure or its foundation," says the harried-looking reporter, her eyes shining with the excitement of being disaster adjacent. "This shutdown could be prolonged if the Titanium Tower is deemed irreparable and must be demolished. The hit this will take on the local economy is yet to be determined, but could go into billions of dollars."

I turn to Matthew. "Bleaters and their money…"

He's not watching telly. He's watching us make breakfast, tears streaming down his face. I set down my knife and go to embrace him. Bridie and Kai notice and do the same, until we're burrowed into each other, and I can smell all our distinct scents, and it's so comforting.

"I'm sorry," Matthew says hoarsely, before clearing his throat. "Watching you all… it was like being home again."

"We'll have that again," Bridie whispers before kissing his cheek. She glances at the stove before breaking away. "Ack! The oatmeal."

She goes back to stirring the pot while Matthew joins Kai over the sausages. I dump the fruit into the pot and start looking for bowls. Luckily, none broke in the quake, so we'll have enough for everyone. That's when I notice Lennon isn't in the kitchen. I go to the dining room, but he's not there, either. I open the door to the living room and find him sweeping glass in front of the fireplace.

"Hey," I call out.

He looks up. "Hey." Then he nods at the mantle. "All the frames fell off and broke."

"Oh, no!"

"It's okay. The pictures are all right."

I go to the coffee table to look at the photos spread across the surface. There are school portraits of Aaron and wedding shots of Tony and May, and a photo of Tony, Lennon, and Aaron on holiday at the beach. Lennon looks about ten years old. He and Aaron are grinning and adorably boyish, while Tony looks stoic and responsible. Being the oldest, I know how that goes, and I feel a twinge of sympathy.

I give a little laugh as I pick it up and hold it out. "Fun fact. I've been in here before, while you were in Seattle, when Kai would come to hang out with Aaron. I even saw this photo, but I didn't realize it was you. Aren't there any newer pictures of you?"

He shrugs. "There were. I guess they got put away after I rebelled." He pauses. "There were photos of Auntie Sylvia, but Tony got rid of those."

Did it all begin with Sylvia, a woman scorned enough to scorch the earth? Or before that, with twin brothers born to parents who hated each other? How do we get past that? "Have you ever blamed Tony and Aaron for what their mother did?"

Lennon stops sweeping. His hands squeeze the broom handle as he takes a deep breath. "Yeah, I did, but it was because they didn't believe that I saw her kill my mother. Now that they do, I don't blame them. But I understand why your family doesn't want me around."

I want to say give them time, but time takes time, and who knows how long it will take? My phone buzzes, startling me. Who would message me that isn't in this house? Maybe Gareth? I pull out my phone.

Christy:Niece, tell your mother to call me. It's urgent.

I roll my eyes and scoff.

"Who is it?" asks Lennon.

"Uncle Christy. He's using the earthquake as an excuse to get Bridie to call him so he can wheedle us back into the Nest. He can sod off. In fact, I'm going to tell him just that."

Penny:Sod off. I know you planned to have me kidnapped. You'll never see me or my family again. I'm blocking you so don't bother replying.

I read the text aloud to Lennon before hitting send. Then, with a strong sense of satisfaction, I block Christy's number. It's followed by another sense, one of loss. I thought my uncle loved me, but he couldn't have. Not if he planned to do that. I shake it off.

"Anyway, breakfast is ready..." I glance at the clock. It's almost noon. "Well, more like brunch at this point. Why don't you join us?"

"When I'm finished here." Lennon goes back to sweeping, meaning he'll come in when we're finished eating.

I sigh. Time is definitely going to take some time.

Back in the kitchen, I get a bowl of oatmeal, top it with a sausage, and pour a cup of coffee. I feel my family's eyes on me as I head back out to the living room. Lennon eyes me as I set the bowl and cup on the table.

"Tuck in," I say, before turning away.

"Thanks," he calls after me.

In the kitchen again, I serve myself, and then hesitate. Half of me wants to join my family in the dining room. The other half wants to join Lennon. Ugh. It. Just. Sucks.

I sit with my family because this will be our first meal together in years. The warmth I feel as I take a seat, surrounded by those I love best, almost makes me forget that half my heart is in the other room.

We're nearly done eating when Aaron comes in and eagerly

scoops up a couple of bowls. "I'm helping May clean up her office. It's a mess. A lot of jars fell and there are herbs and sh…" He takes a quick glance at my parents. "and stuff everywhere."

"May's a doctor," Kai explains to Matthew, before turning again to his friend. "You guys need help?" Aaron nods. Kai gets up. "I'll carry the coffee."

"Cool. Thanks."

As they leave, Cat and Roy show up and take their food to go as well, with thanks, but no explanation. Maybe they need some alone time.

Last to arrive is Tony, and he walks right past the food. "Where is Lennon?"

"In the living room," I reply.

He strides out the door without another word.

Our table becomes silent as we exchange worried glances. Then Bridie whispers, "I hope nothing's wrong."

"Why are you whispering?" I whisper back.

She glares at me before turning to Matthew. "See what I had to put up with while you were gone?" Her phone buzzes on the tabletop. She turns it over with a sigh and stares at the screen. Then her brow knits.

"Christy?" asks Matthew.

"No. Joanne." She tilts the screen so we can both read the message from Christy's wife.

CALL!!!

We exchange troubled looks. Joanne, as Mother Bird of the local Nest, wouldn't abuse her power by engaging in a sham, not even to aid her husband.

"Something must be wrong," I say. "Maybe someone got hurt in the quake."

"That's what I'm thinking. I better call." She gives her head a defiant toss. "Actually, there's no reason all of us can't hear what Christy has to say."

She places her phone on the coffee table and taps the screen so the speaker is on. It rings only once before Christy answers.

"Bridie?" Is there a tremble in his voice?

"Yes, Christy. What do you want? Is everyone all right?"

"We're fine. It's not any of us." There's a long pause. "Are you sitting down, love?"

Now she pauses. A tense silence fills the room. My stomach clenches.

"Yes, I'm sitting. What's wrong?"

His voice drops to a husky whisper. "It's the mirror, Bridie. It broke in the earthquake."

Time stands still. A small aftershock rattles the building, but none of us moves.

"Bridie?" My uncle's voice comes from the bottom of a well.

Color drains from Bridie's face. She blinks and stares blankly, as if unable to speak.

I jump to my feet and grab the phone. "What are you going on about, Uncle Christy? Are you trying to sham us?"

"I wouldn't sham about that, girl. Your mother knows."

"How could it break? Didn't you keep it somewhere safe?"

"Too right, I did! Wrapped in foam and locked in my strongbox. Safe from thieves, fire, and flood, but not an earthquake. Look."

The phone buzzes as a text arrives. I tap on it. Christy has sent a photo of the mirror, cracked in half, lipstick and blood smeared on its surface.

My hand clamps my mouth to keep from screaming. Tears fill my eyes.

Matthew takes the phone from me and shows Bridie. Her pain-filled gasp hurts my ears. Christy is still talking, but Matthew hangs up on him.

I find my voice again. "Did she tell you about Kingfisher and the curse?"

He nods grimly. Then he sits beside Bridie, taking her limp white hand. "Are you sure this curse is real? Do you know anyone who's ever used it, that it's ever worked?"

She comes to life with a painful gasp. "It's real. All too real." Tears fill her eyes and spill down her cheeks. "I've got you back. I've got my children, my family. And now it's over. My joy cut short." She smears her hand across her face as she sniffles. "But I don't care. I'd do it again, twice over, to keep that man away from my family."

As she speaks, my fingers work nervously at the Yin Pearl, its low-key thrum tingling my skin. This power, this healing energy, can I use it for curses? I close my eyes and delve into its depths, following the flow of what I can heal using the Dragon Touch. Diseases, broken bones, and yes, curses. It'd be miraculous, god-like, if it weren't for the fact that every malady removed must be cast into another. Karma floats on the surface, a reminder that whatever is done must be paid for in-kind.

I speak as if in a daze, still amidst the pearl. "Mum, don't cry. Don't be afraid. I can heal you."

She blinks her red-rimmed eyes. "What do you mean, heal me? You mean, the same way you healed Matty?"

"Yes, with Lennon's help."

But there's a catch. There always is with karma and magic.

Lennon

Dragons don't wait and neither do earthquakes. They don't care if you've had enough sleep or if you've got important things to do, like keeping your family alive. At least they can't keep me from eating, though I gobble my oatmeal before something else can happen.

As I sip my coffee, I reach out, seeking a certain serpentine presence. I don't have to go far. Jade Dragon coils around one of the Bay Bridge towers, scrutinizing the traffic jam below.

Why do they continue to press the horns of their vehicles? he asks. *What good does it do?*

Humans get frustrated when they're scared and can't move. Honking their horns helps them relieve the frustration.

He squints. *It seems an act of aggression, meant to anger one another.*

I shrug. I can't argue with that. *So, you like the earthquake?*

He doesn't speak, but he makes this hissing sound, similar to a purr, indicating he digs it the most because this is his thing. Dragons love observing chaos and all its possibilities.

Hey, I had a dream about you.

I have dreamt of you as well.

I never think of dragons sleeping or dreaming. *Where do you sleep?*

Where I find shelter.

Do you have a home?

My home is where I will.

What does that even mean? There's no point in asking, but there is something I want to know. *What did you dream about me?*

That you become what you will be.

You mean the Dragon Son?

He doesn't answer because he wants me to use my wisdom to figure it out and breaks contact with me because he's done.

The dining room door swings open and Tony strides in like he's the boss and I'm bullshit. Same old, same old.

"Did you eat?" I ask. "Bridie makes tasty oatmeal."

His grim expression doesn't change, as if I hadn't spoken. Guess he's not hungry. He sits in his chair before asking, "Where is Jade Dragon?"

"Here. In the city, I mean. Hanging out."

"He's here to observe. To see who will prevail."

I mean, that's pretty much what Jade Dragon does in any situation, so, "Yeah."

"Jeremiah Walks Long called. The Beggars stationed near the 88 took photos while the building was being evacuated after the earthquake." As Tony speaks, he swipes his phone before handing it to me.

On screen, there's a photo of a crowd gathered outside the building. Nothing remarkable, except one man looks familiar. I zoom in on his face and gasp. "Uncle George?"

Tony nods once.

"What's he doing there?"

"He's come for us and the pearls. He won't leave any of us alive."

Saves us the trouble of going to Hong Kong. Cool, I guess.

Except he must feel pretty confident coming here to take us on. Or maybe impatient. He's been playing the long game for a long time.

I puff myself up with a confidence I don't really feel. "Fine. Bring it. We've got two pearls, he's got one. We'll toast his ass."

"He's also got two pearls. The Wisdom and the Summoning Pearls."

"So? The Summoning Pearl summons Jade Dragon, and he's already here."

"He also has the manual for the Wisdom Pearl. It may contain the knowledge of using those pearls together. Think about it. Think of how he's summoned so many to his side."

Well, shit. I rub my chin. "Would this be a good time to attack? I mean, since he's out in the open."

"No. Although the building has an evacuation order, the Traitor used his powers to circumvent it. He's entrenched on the twenty-eighth floor." Tony pauses as he pulls his buzzing phone from his pocket. His frown deepens as he stares at the screen. "It's Jeremiah."

Has Uncle George made a move? "Put it on speaker."

Tony taps the screen and sets the phone on the coffee table. "Beggar Chief."

Jeremiah's smoky voice has an irritated rasp. "Mad Maud called. She said the kids disappeared last night."

My brother and I exchange glances and nods. It's in Jeremiah's best interest not to betray us. I reply, "Hey, it's me. We're here, me and Penny, in the *kongsi*. We traveled secretly, so my uncle doesn't know we've left London."

"What the hell? You disappeared without telling anyone and left me and Mad Maud holding the bag?"

Pretty much, but I don't say that aloud.

"You want our help? Stop sneaking around like a goddamn cat. You should've informed me the moment you returned to SF."

"We've been a little busy," I draw out the Y. "I don't know if you noticed, but there was an earthquake."

"Pull your head out of your ass, kid. Your uncle's holed up in the 88 without a lot of backup. I'm not gonna waste this opportunity. We attack today."

"What do you mean, we…" I start to ask, but Tony holds up his hand before I can finish.

"If you attack our enemy, Beggar Chief, that's your decision. We won't join you until we're ready."

There's a moment of stony silence before the Almighty Head of the Crossroads valiantly states, "No. We attack together or not at all."

"What's your price for joining forces with us?" asks Tony.

Jeremiah answers without hesitation. "One hundred years added to your agreement with Mad Maud."

"Screw that," I burst out.

Tony holds up his hand again and shoots me a glare before saying, "No."

Another silence, long enough for Jeremiah to consider what he's got to lose if we lose. Namely, the entire Crossroads, because Uncle George won't hold back once he's got all the pearls. He clears his throat before saying, "You'll acknowledge me as leader of the battle and the victory will be mine."

I physically gag.

"Done," says Tony. He taps the screen to hang up.

"Can you believe that?" I sneer. "What a wanker."

My brother's gaze is not patient. "You need to respond to our allies in a manner befitting the Dragon Son."

There are so many things I could say, like, why should I when you're the real Dragon Son? Or, if John Walks Long was alive, we wouldn't have to put up with this petty bullshit. None of it will help, so I choose silence.

The dining-room door opens and Penny walks in.

I grin. "You're not gonna believe what Jeremiah just said."

"Jeremiah?" she repeats as if she doesn't know him. Then I notice her clenched hands and distracted gaze.

I stand. "What's wrong?"

"Am I interrupting?" she asks in a breathy tone so unlike her.

"No. We just got off the phone with Jeremiah. He told us that Uncle George… I mean, the Traitor, is in San Francisco."

Her eyes widen. "What's he doing here?"

Tony answers, "Waiting for you and Lennon to return so he can attack and seize the pearls."

"Does he know we're back?"

"Not yet."

She exhales, but not with relief, and mutters, "Bollocks," before turning to me. "The mirror cracked."

My mouth drops open. Oh. Shit. "The earthquake?"

She nods.

"Can we use the pearls to heal her?" I ask.

She nods again, her expression unchanged, as if there's something more, but she can't tell me aloud. "Can you join us? Both of you?"

"Yeah. Give us a sec."

After she leaves, I explain to a perplexed Tony. I never told him the whole story about how Bridie cast a blood curse to prevent Kingfisher from pursuing us, and how she gave the mirror to Christy to keep Kingfisher from retaking the Nest.

Tony gives a sage nod. "A powerful curse has powerful consequences."

"Yeah, well, not as powerful as me and Penny. We can take on a curse. Don't let Jeremiah know or he'll want credit."

In the dining room, Penny sits with her parents, her fingers knitting her hands into a tight ball. Matthew has his arm around Bridie while muttering words of comfort. Her cheeks are wet, her eyes brimming with unshed tears.

"Where's Kai?" I ask. "Should we wait for him?"

"No!" Bridie sits up and out of Matthew's embrace. "I don't want Kai to know. He just got his father back. I don't want him to worry about losing his mother. He's living in enough fear already."

Matthew frowns. "I don't want to lie to him."

"We're not lying. We're simply not telling him something he doesn't need to know..."

"Mum," Penny interrupts. "I think he needs to know."

Steel enters Bridie's tone. "No. I'm his mother and I make that choice. Besides," she turns to Tony, "shouldn't we keep this as secret as possible?"

"Yes," he replies without hesitation. "Since you're using the power of the pearls, this must be on a need-to-know basis. Aaron is too young to be involved and we know he'll tell Kai. However, Auntie Cat and Uncle Roy could be useful, so we'll include them."

You know times are strange when Tony and Bridie become allies. Personally, I don't think it's a good idea to exclude Aaron and Kai. As Dragon Son, I could override Tony, but this isn't his curse. It's Bridie's and if she doesn't want them involved, what can I do?

"The curse will remain in the pearl until you cast it into someone else, correct?" Tony asks Penny.

"That's what happened in London," she replies. "I cast Matthew's illness into the assassin who came to kill us."

"Can you cast the curse into the Traitor?"

Now, that's a damn fine idea. It would solve all our problems without shedding a drop of blood... well, Kingfisher and Uncle George will still die, but that's totally cool.

"You mean from here, without him anywhere nearby?" She rubs her chin. "I don't know. I think I need him to be present, or at least close enough that I can sense his energy." She turns to me. "Can we go somewhere private and see if we can figure it out?"

"There's a spare bedroom we can use. Right?" I ask Tony. He doesn't reply, so I take it as a reserved yes.

We stand and I can feel their eyes bore into us as we leave the room. What do they think we're going to do when we're alone? I hope they trust us enough to know how bad the situation is.

Thing is, as soon as we're in the hall and realize there's no one else around, her hand slips into mine. It feels so good: soft, cool, strong. I lead us into an unused guest room at the end of the next corridor, close the door, turn on the lights, and it's just us, alone at last.

Penny slides into my arms, laying her cheek on my shoulder. I wrap my arms around her and hold her tight. She's not trembling, but I can sense the fear coursing through her.

"What is it?" I whisper. "Can't you heal Bridie?"

"I can," she whispers back. "But when I remove the curse, I'll be taking a piece of her soul along with it."

Penny

"Are you sure?" Lennon asks.

I nod against his shoulder. "Magic demands a price of the soul. The worse the curse, the deeper the cut."

"Maybe we can heal that, too."

Can we? I want to believe it, but I know better. I let go of him and step away, clutching my elbows to keep from shivering. "The power of the pearls comes from a dragon. We'd need fairy magic to heal her soul."

"Aren't you part-fairy? Maybe that fairy part of you can heal Bridie's soul."

"This isn't about healing." I pace. "It's about a price that Bridie must pay if she's to be rid of the curse. We need to heal her as soon as Kingfisher dies. Once the curse passes into her, she's doomed. Anything could kill her. And the sooner we remove the curse, the less of a grip it will have on her soul."

"Do you know where he is?"

I stop and shake my head. "Even if we did, there's no way we can know the exact moment of his death."

His face goes owlish. Not sweet, but predatory. "Yeah, there is."

"How?"

"We kill him ourselves."

I blink, but don't think before saying, "We can't. We have to be here to heal Bridie."

"No, I mean, I'll put out a hit on him."

"Do you know how to do that?"

"No, but I'm sure Tony does."

We stare at each other for a few silent moments before I say, "Is it bad we decided that so easily?"

"I don't know if bad is the right word." He rubs the Yang Pearl beneath his shirt. "It's, like, since I've worn this, I've become more ruthless or something. Does that sound right?"

I nod slowly. "Yeah. I thought wearing the Yin Pearl would make me, I don't know. More compassionate, I guess, since it's for healing, but it's kinda done the opposite. I can't be arsed about killing Kingfisher or your uncle. I didn't want to be this murder-y, but..." I shrug.

"Hey, they'd kill us and have dinner next to our dead bodies, so..." He shrugs, too.

"Then let's figure out how we're going to do all this." I hold up my hands and close my eyes. His palms press into mine and I feel the calluses on his skin, as he must feel mine. Are similar calluses growing in our hearts, like dragon scales? What does that make us? Less human? More than human? It doesn't matter. I'll make any transformation necessary to save my mother.

Together, we inhale. Exhale all other thoughts. Inhale as we tap into the core of our pearls. Exhale as we send that energy into each other until it becomes a single stream of power and we become one. As we do, I think of what Matthew said, how he used the Yin Pearl to leave his body.

I want to try, I say. *Maybe, together, I'll have more power.*

All right. His reply is like a whisper across my soul.

But how to do it? Matthew was in an altered state of

consciousness. His body was stuck, but his mind was free to roam. I'm firmly within myself and that self fears separation from my body.

Don't be afraid. I have you and I'll bring you back.

I know.

I do know. I'm not alone. Not even as I let go and lift out of my body. I'm floating, except not really. I just… am. My presence without form. I can see, crystal clear, clearer than life, but I have no other physical sensation. I can't feel the fear I should experience looking at my body without me in it. What I do feel is the power of the Yin and Yang pearls channeled through the dyad that is me and Lennon. Using that power, I propel myself through the thick wooden grain of the door.

In the hall, I seek the energy of others and find them. Tony, in the living room, talking on the phone. May, in the nursery, staring at the empty crib. Kai and Aaron, in the kitchen, blissfully unaware as they go back for more sausages. Cat and Roy in his bedroom, holding hands and talking. Finally, Bridie and Matthew in their bedroom, holding hands, but not talking.

I sense the curse, a malignancy in her soul that will continue growing until we cut it out. It's a malevolent thing, full of pain, bitterness, and fury. Not just what she felt against Kingfisher, but what she felt against the world for putting her in that position. I need to slow the growth, but how?

Leannán Sidhe gave her descendants the power to bless and curse. A blessing, then. But which one? As I think this, I feel a gentle glow spark within the Yin Pearl. Words come to me without thought, flowing through me like a stream. I sing, though I have no voice and hear no tune.

> *May the blessings of day be upon you,*
> *Light without and light within.*
> *May the blessings of night be upon you,*
> *Dark without and dark within.*

Day and night, protect you,
From the evil without and within.

I see Bridie gasp and press a hand to her chest. A look of peace comes over her face, as if she can sense that the growth has stopped.

Temporarily.

The blessing should hold until Kingfisher dies and she must face the full consequences of her curse.

I retreat as though a slow but powerful vacuum was sucking me in, across the hall, through the door, and back into my body. My head spins and my knees collapse. Lennon catches me as I sag against him. He lifts me into his arms and carries me to the bed, laying me down, and hovering over me with a worried expression. "Are you okay?"

"Yeah. That was weird. Coming back into my body was a real head rush. How are you?"

"The usual. Drained, but, okay."

I pat the space on the bed beside me. Lennon lays down and we hold hands. I close my eyes and pretend we're on the cot in his studio, but the room is too warm, the bed too comfortable, and there's no smell of paint or background bustle of artists and makers. I feel Lennon sigh and I'm pretty sure he's thinking the same thing, but there's no time for that now.

I roll over to face him, leaning on my elbow. "How much of that did you feel?"

He rolls over as well. So close. So kissable, especially when that owlish look comes over his face. "All of it, I guess. You did something."

"I blessed her."

"Yeah, but that wasn't just a blessing. There was power involved. Like, you could use your power even though you were a spirit."

I think for a moment about how it felt. My blessing stopped the curse from growing. That took power. "Maybe using the pearls together enables me to use our powers, even though I'm astral projecting."

We stare at each other for a moment, considering the possibilities.

"This could be huge," he finally says.

"Yeah, but we better make sure before we say anything."

"Now?"

"Now is good."

We sit cross-legged on the bed, knees touching as we face each other. Our hands clasp as my eyes close. I delve into the Yin Pearl, becoming one with its energy, and feel Lennon's presence in the flow of the Yang Pearl. As our *chi* combine, my body releases its hold on my soul.

It's easier this time, since I know what to expect. I'm also more aware of Lennon's presence, that he's with me through the Yang Pearl. What I don't feel is that tether that Matthew spoke. Maybe I haven't gone far enough. I propel myself upward, through the ceiling and onto the next floor. It's dark, except for a few hall lights, although it seems similar in layout to the second floor.

Is this where you grew up? I ask.

Yeah. I feel rather than hear his tone. He doesn't want to be here. Too many memories of a murdered mother and a ruined father.

So I float through the ceiling and onto the rooftop. Armed guards stand watch, all of them wearing headphones to keep from being seduced by George Lau's power of persuasion. I keep going into the sky, and still no tether. Maybe the combined power of the Yin and Yang Pearls keeps me from breaking free and floating away. The view is incredible. I can see the Bay Bridge, the Golden Gate Bridge, and the city spread out below me. Heavy traffic fills the major streets and hampers emergency vehicles. Plumes of gray and white smoke rise from a fire to the south. Wisps of fog pass through me. Seagulls avoid me, as if aware of my presence.

Hey, don't go too far, says Lennon.

He's right. It's hard not to be seduced by this freedom, but not at the cost of losing myself entirely. I propel myself back down, into Chinatown, and above the roof of the *kongsi.* That's when I notice a drone hovering above the building. A guard with a pellet gun attempts to shoot it down, but its erratic movements make it a hard target.

Shall we? I ask.

Let's, says Lennon.

As the guard shoots his gun, Lennon's power surges through me. I aim it at the drone and miss as it drops and swerves. I drop as well as my energy wanes. Lennon boosts me with his *chi,* but I can tell this is taking a toll on him, too. I dig deep into both our reservoirs. There's enough left for one more shot.

I concentrate on the flow of energy coming from the drone. The guard shoots several more times and I duck and swerve along with the drone, like we're dancing on a firing range, until we're in sync. The guard shoots again and I take my shot. My dance partner disintegrates. Little drone pieces rain down on the building. The guards cheer and high-five the guy with the gun.

My flow of energy sputters to a halt as if someone pulled the plug. The vacuum yanks me out of the sky, through the building, and back into my body. My eyes pop open and I suck in air, pressing my hand to my pounding heart.

"Whoa," Lennon gasps. "That's a head rush."

I take a few moments to catch my breath before asking, "How much did you see?"

He frowns. "I don't know if 'see' is the right word. I saw nothing, but I felt everything. Does that make sense?"

"I guess. I mean, you know we took out the drone."

"Yeah."

"But that took everything out of us. It's going to take a lot more power to cast the curse into George."

"You don't think we can do it?"

"I didn't say that. I just don't know how. Yet."

"We'll figure it out. We should tell everyone."

"Yeah." I try sitting up and collapse back against the pillows. Lennon does the same. "I think we need to rest for a few minutes."

"Yeah," he sighs.

We snuggle into each other like we do at the studio, all warm and comforting. I close my eyes, breathe in his familiar scent, and fall asleep.

A knock on the door awakens me. Lennon stirs and grumbles without answering. I'm tempted to do the same, until I hear Bridie say, "Can I come in?"

"Hold on a sec." I roll off the bed and stand with firm legs, my *chi* having regained its steady flow. I go to the door, crack it open, and slide out so we don't disturb Lennon. "What's up?"

"Just wanted to let you two know that dinner will be ready soon." Her eyes are full of forlorn hope. She needs to hear something, anything, that will keep her going.

"Can we talk?" I ask. "Privately, I mean."

Her face falls. "Is it bad?"

Do I sugarcoat reality for her? No. This is too important. "There's an issue we need to discuss."

"All right," she breathes out. "Let's go to the nursery."

We enter the room full of Lennon's joyful pink dolphins and sit on the bed. Bridie wrings her hands as she waits for me to spell her doom. There's no way to say it but to say it.

"We can heal you, but there's a catch. When we remove the curse, it will cut out a piece of your soul."

Her mouth forms an O. Then she inhales sharply, blinks,

and exhales as she says, "Of course. A mirror curse is a soul curse. It could be any part of my soul, couldn't it? It could be something simple, like my love of apples, or something more noticeable, like my love of the Beatles, or, or..." She goes still as dread washes over her face. Her voice lowers to a hoarse whisper as tears fill her eyes. "Or it could be my love for Matthew."

That same dread fills me. I want to reassure her, but I can't. "It could be any of those things or something else. We don't know."

"I just got him back. I... I... I love him now more than ever. I can't lose that. I'd rather die."

"Mum, no. Don't say that. Think about how Matthew would feel."

"I am. Imagine him looking in my eyes and no longer seeing love."

That would be awful. The worst. No. The worst would be her dying for nothing. "Mum, you don't know what's going to happen. Think of Kai. How will he feel if his mother dies without at least trying to live?"

She gasps, clutching her heart. "What if I lose my love for my children?"

She's spiraling, clawing away at the protection surrounding the curse. I take a deep breath and take her tense, icy hand as I tap into that strange mixture of Yin Pearl healing and fairy blessing. I sing aloud; the tune coming to me now, though I couldn't hear it as a spirit. It sounds ancient and more of a chant than a song.

> *"May the blessings of day be upon you,*
> *Light without and light within."*

Bridie lifts her head and joins me, her voice pure and clear.

"May the blessings of night be upon you,
Dark without and dark within.
Day and night, protect you,
From the evil without and within."

As we finish, we exhale. A sense of peace fills the room, like sunlight on a cloudy day. Bridie squeezes my hand before letting go to wipe away her tears.

I keep my voice gentle. "Do you know where Kingfisher is?"

She shakes her head. "No, but Christy will. Why?"

"I can't heal you until the fullness of the curse is upon you and that will only happen after he dies."

"I'll call Christy." She gives a resolute nod. "Leannán Sidhe has spoken. She'll take what she must, but won't leave me forsaken."

I don't know that I trust Leannán Sidhe that much. Whatever she tries taking from my mother, I'm going to fight her for.

Lennon

She walks through my dreams, a woman with long black hair, silver eyes, pointy ears, and dressed in flowing silken robes blue as the sky at twilight. She looks young, as young as me, and so beautiful I'd lose my heart to her if I wasn't already in love with Penny. Her song beckons me as she walks the path of a labyrinth toward the center, where I'm to join her…

"Lennon." Penny's whisper draws me away, back to her, back to life.

I blink, trying to remember what I dreamt. It all seemed so real, but now, with Penny standing beside the bed, it fades into whatever abyss dreams go.

"Sorry to wake you," she says as she sits cross-legged beside me.

"It's okay." I rub my eyes as I sit up. "I was dreaming…"

"About Gerry?"

"No." I frown. Was it? Somehow, it feels like it was, but… I grasp at the remaining threads before shaking my head. It's gone. "Is everything okay? How's Bridie?"

"Terrified. I'm trying not to be terrified, too."

"You mean about the soul thing?"

"Yeah. I don't know what part of her soul she's going to lose. It could be anything…" A knock on the door interrupts her. She huffs with exasperation before calling out, "What?"

Aaron and Kai slide in, close the door, and hop on the bed to join us.

Kai flops back on the mattress before asking, "What's the craic?"

"Bugger off," says his sister.

"Why? What are you guys doing?"

Aaron nudges me with his elbow. "Tony thinks you're being irresponsible and hanging out with Penny when you should be doing… I dunno. Everything?"

I roll my eyes. "Then Tony can be the fucking Dragon Son."

"I guess. He'd be better at it than you."

"I know, right?"

"What do you want?" asks Penny.

"We're done helping May and we're bored," says Kai.

"Yeah. Tony took away our phones so my dad… I mean, the Traitor, whatever, can't call us and do that talking mojo thing he does."

"We told him we won't answer the phone, but he doesn't believe us," Kai gripes.

"Dude," says Aaron, "I told you Tony doesn't do belief." He tugs at his Rocket Man T-shirt, featuring Elton John all decked out in feathers and a boa. Kai unconsciously mimics his action, tugging at his David Bowie lightning bolt T-shirt.

Man, I would've loved to wear T-shirts like that when I was their age, but my parents would've reamed me. Who knew Tony would be so permissive? I mean, music lessons, art school, a cool Crossroads friend, everything I'd wanted and couldn't have until I ran away. Then again, Tony's been so busy keeping everything together that maybe he didn't have time to discipline Aaron like he did me. Is anyone even checking in with him, and making sure he's okay with all the shit that's been happening?

"Hey," I say to Aaron. "You okay?"

His goofy mask slips into a frown. "What d'ya mean?"

"I mean, are you okay?"

He stares at me long enough that I don't think he's going to answer, then blurts out, "Yeah, I'm great. I mean, aside from my mom killing your mom, and my dad killing your dad, and finding out that Tony is my brother AND my cousin. And I can't go to school or even go outside because my dad - excuse me - the Traitor," He uses air quotes, "wants to kidnap me and, I dunno, force me to be his evil minion. Other than that, yeah, it's all good." His arms fold tight across his chest. "Oh, and my uncle almost killed my best friend's dad. There's that, too."

Well, shit.

If there's anyone I didn't want all this to affect, it's him. How stupid is that because how could it not?

Kai nudges Aaron. "Dude, none of that's your fault. Besides, I have a shitty murder family, too. My grandparents tried to kill Penny and Lennon."

"All because of those stupid pearls. What good are they, anyway, if all they do is make people kill each other?" Aaron turns to me again. "I don't blame you for wanting to run away."

I fight to keep the guilt from my expression. "What do you mean? I'm here."

"Yeah, for now, but Tony says you're gonna dump the pearls on him and run away with Penny when this is all done."

"He told you that?"

"No, he told May. I overheard them talking. You want my advice? Do that. Leave the pearls here and run for it. That's the only way Tony will accept them."

He's right, except for one thing. Penny gives me an apologetic glance before saying, "No one's running away. Once this is over, Mum and Ba want to go back to London and pick up where they left off, and Kai and I are going with them."

"I don't want to go back," says Kai.

Her head whips around to face him. "What?"

He shrugs. "I want to stay here. I like my school and my teachers, and me and Aaron wanna form a band."

"You're already in a band. Our band."

"I can be in more than one." His face becomes defensive.

Penny folds her arms. "How can you not want to go back to London?"

Kai gives another, tighter shrug. "London's cool, but it always got weird when we'd leave. People stared at us."

"People will stare at us here if we leave San Francisco."

"You don't get it. It's hard for people like me on the Crossroads."

"You mean biracial?"

"No. Bi…" He bites his lip and looks down before mumbling, "Nothing."

Aaron squirms beside him. Then he leans in and whispers loud enough for us to hear, "Dude, let's just tell them." Kai hunches his shoulders without replying. "You said you were ready."

"Maybe I'm not," Kai mumbles.

"What if we all die and we never told no one? We should at least tell them."

"You sure?"

"Yeah."

Kai squints at us. "I guess they won't judge."

"Tell us what?" asks Penny.

"Judge what?" I ask.

They exchange wary, worried glances and take deep breaths.

"I'm bisexual," says Kai.

"And I'm gay," says Aaron.

I feel my face go blank. Then I stare at their T-shirts. Talk about hiding in plain sight. How did I not know this? I've known Aaron his whole life. I remember when he was born. Spent most of my life being the second boss of him. Then I went away for two years and ghosted him. I wasn't there when he started making realizations about himself, realizations he knew he'd have to keep hidden.

Penny's face also goes blank before a puzzled frown appears. "Why didn't you tell me?"

Kai shrugs. "I wasn't sure. I mean, I dig chicks, so I thought maybe I was straight, except I also dig dudes."

"And I just dig dudes," says Aaron. "I wasn't sure, either, and kinda hoping I'd start liking girls, but I don't. I mean, I like them, but not like that."

Penny's frown remains aimed at her brother. "That doesn't explain why you didn't tell me. You know I'd support you. Mum, too."

He glances at Aaron, who says, "We're keeping it secret cuz we don't want Tony to find out, cuz then he'll think Kai ruined me, the same way he thinks you ruined Lennon."

"What?" Penny huffs. "I didn't ruin anybody." Her brow wrinkles. "Wait. Are you two… um… together?"

The boys shake their heads without looking at each other.

"We're not with anyone," says Kai. "We're trying to figure stuff out and we can't do that if I'm in London and Aaron's here, and we don't know anyone else gay on the Crossroads."

Am I a bad person that my heart lifts at the thought of Penny staying in SF because her brother's in the closet?

Her expression gentles. "You know someone. Gareth. He'll gladly help you figure it out. And Aaron can come visit and stay as long as he wants."

"I really miss Pa," says Kai wistfully. "But I wanna finish school. You got to graduate. Why can't I?"

"You can go to school in London. No one's stopping you."

Kai crosses his arms. "It's not the same and you know it."

She gives an exasperated sigh, even though I can tell from her expression it isn't the same and she knows it.

"Aaron." I wait until he lifts his head to look me in the eye with an uncertain gaze. "Thank you for telling me. I totally support you. You know that, right?"

"I guess, I mean, I knew if anyone would, it'd be you. And Auntie Cat. But everyone else?" He scoffs.

"I don't know. I think Uncle Roy would be cool with it. May won't care. Tony…" I draw out his name. "I don't think he cares about people being gay."

"People," Aaron points out glumly. "I'm not people. I'm his little brother. He's gonna ream me."

"Maybe not. I mean, he might not be happy at first, but he'll get over it. He's not a homophobe." At least, I hope he isn't. Pretty sure he's not.

"Is it bad being gay in the Two Dragon Clan?" asks Penny.

"Not like with Strowlers," I reply. "It's like a don't ask, don't tell situation. They don't get married and instead hang out with a special friend," I make air quotes, "and everyone says they're," I think of the best translation, "soul mates, but in a martial arts sense, like, platonic."

"So, denial."

"Pretty much."

"I don't wanna live in denial," says Aaron. "I wanna be out and proud and march in the parade."

"Yeah. Out and proud," proclaims Kai.

"We want that for you, too," says Penny. "Why did you decide to tell us now?"

Aaron shrugs. "There are so many secrets and most of them ruined our family. I don't want to keep this secret any longer than I gotta."

"I'm glad you told us." Penny turns to her brother. "You

need to tell Mum and Ba. Things are…" She exhales. "Things aren't great right now. Anything could happen."

"You mean, like, someone could die?" he asks.

"I think she means we could all die," says Aaron. "And we shouldn't keep this a secret cuz our families should know."

"Something like that." She chews her lip as if biting back more words.

I know how she feels. They just spilled their guts, and we're keeping a major secret from them. It's taking all my willpower not to blurt out everything about the mirror. This sucks. They deserve to know, especially Kai.

There's a sharp rap on the door before it swings open. Tony strides in and the boys shrink back like guilty cats. He stares down at us like we're massive fuckups before announcing, "Dinnertime." Then he strides back out, leaving the door wide open.

I exhale. Maybe it is better they don't know. They've got enough going on dealing with their own secrets. Aaron's right. Tony won't take it well and he will blame Penny, Kai, and me for leading Aaron onto the Wayward Way. All that can wait until after they find out Bridie lost a piece of her soul, and that Penny and I used that piece to kill Aaron's father.

Lennon

After dinner, May turns to Aaron and Kai and says, "I need you two to come with me to the main kitchen and help bring food to the guards on the roof."

As an excuse, it's just okay, especially since Aaron immediately squints in confusion. "I thought the kitchen staff served the guards."

She looks at him with stern eyes and lips pressed thin. "No one is too good for any task in this family or clan."

He ducks his head. "Okay."

Kai looks at him like he's an idiot. Then he turns on the Irish charm with a bright smile. "May, d'ya mind if we hang out on the roof for a while? Get some fresh air."

May turns to Tony, who nods and says, "As long as you obey the commands of the guards."

The boys nod vigorously and follow May out the door. As I watch them leave, I wonder if Mom did that to me, sent me on some pointless errand to keep me ignorant of the mess she and Dad were drowning in. I'm sure she did. As if that ignorance did me any good.

Bridie exhales as if some small part of her burden has been

relieved. Mom must've done the same, thinking she was protecting me. Would I be an asshole if I pointed that out to Bridie? Probably.

Penny waits until the door closes behind them before saying, "We experimented with the pearls. We can remove the curse, but casting it into George is another issue." She explains about using astral projection and taking out the drone. "So, we have the ability, but we don't have enough power. And we can't do it from here. We need to be a lot closer to where he is."

"I can help," says Auntie Cat. "Some of the power of the Yang Pearl still resides within me, and..." She looks down, licking her lips before speaking again. "And when I wore the pearl, I used its power to cast an evil spell into someone, killing them."

Everyone freezes, except Roy, who bows his head. Of course, he knows. So many shared secrets between them, just like me and Penny. I don't want to end up like them, holding it all in for twenty years. All that stuff needs to come out now so we can move forward. "Who did you kill?" I ask.

"Your grandmother, my father's First Wife."

My mouth drops open. Well. Shit. Do these pearls turn everyone into killers? Since I'm about to off my uncle, I'm not feeling super judge-y about her killing my grandmother, but I need to know. "Why?"

Tony speaks before she can reply. "I was told she died right after my parents..." His lips press tight for a moment. "Right after the Traitor and my mother were married. That she died of a heart attack, and everyone considered it a bad omen for their marriage."

Well, they were sure as hell right about that.

Auntie Cat sucks in a hard breath. "The morning of the wedding, I found out that Tiffany, your grandmother, had hired assassins to kill my mother, and cast an evil spell slowly killing my father. She'd planned to claim George had been born first and that he was the true Dragon Son."

"Who told you?" asks Tony, still not blinking, but gripping the table.

"Sylvia."

Now he blinks. "My mother?"

"Yes. She wanted to stop the wedding, so she sent me a note that led me to the proof of what had happened. By then, I was wearing the Yang Pearl and Jade Dragon confirmed everything."

"Jade Dragon sent you to kill our grandmother?"

"No. He doesn't send you to do things, but he gives you the power to do them if that's your decision, which he did for me."

"Yeah," I say aloud before I can stop myself. "That's exactly what he does."

Tony side-eyes me before declaring, "So, you killed her?"

Auntie Cat closes her eyes and exhales before nodding. "I used the Yang Pearl to cast the entirety of the spell into her. I thought I could save my father, but it was too late. He died soon after."

"Who else knew of this?"

Uncle Roy lifts his head. "Me and Mike. No one else. Mike had found out about his mother's plans from Sylvia. He was going to kill her himself, but Cat beat him to it. He didn't want the rest of the clan to find out about the attempted coup and believed anyone else who might've been involved would take her death as a warning. We thought that was the end of it, but we were wrong."

"So, all this stuff between Dad and Uncle… and his brother, it's been going on since then?" I ask.

Auntie Cat shakes her head. "It's been going on since Mike and George were born. They were set up to be rivals from day one. You two need to stop blaming yourselves. This has nothing to do with you. It's always been about them. Mike's death didn't end it. George won't stop until he's the Dragon Son." She sighs as she rubs her forehead. "I wish I'd realized it sooner. He hadn't been part of his mother's scheme and I think if Mike hadn't slept with Sylvia and fathered Tony, her death would've been the end. Something snapped after he found out, but he kept it well hidden. I think what finally made him act was when he found out Mike planned to replace Lennon with Tony as his heir. He must've got hold of the Wisdom Pearl by then, which gave him the power to move on his mother's plans."

My grandmother sounds a lot like Auntie Sylvia. It's kind of sad that their only way to power was secondhand, through men who didn't love or even care about them. I don't blame Auntie Cat for killing her since I would've done the same thing. I'm about to say so, but Tony speaks up.

"She died a traitor's death and so will her son. We must set things right before our clan is destroyed. Can you help Lennon and Penny channel the curse into the Traitor?"

"Yes," she says without hesitation. "But like Penny said, we can't do it from here. We must get close to George."

"How close?"

"The closer, the better."

We turn to Penny and her parents, who sat in wide-eyed silence through the story of my grandmother's treachery and death. I think we're winning again in terms of whose family is more fucked up.

She clears her throat. "Um, I don't think we'll know 'til we're there, but getting our energy boosted should help with that."

"All we lack is the curse." Tony turns to Bridie. "Will you know when it enters you?"

She shakes her head. "There's no lore on it, so I can't say."

"Did Uncle Christy tell you where Kingfisher is?" asks Penny.

Bridie nods, "He's in Las Vegas, in a Bleater trailer park next to the Sports City Casino. According to Christy, he's plotting to take over the Strowler Nest there."

Penny and I exchange glances. It's our turn to add another murder to the growing list. I take a deep breath. "The best time for us to remove the curse is when it first enters Bridie, and the only way we can do that is if we know the exact moment when Kingfisher dies, so…"

"We kill him ourselves," interrupts Tony.

Trust him to steal my murder thunder. "Yeah."

"I'll do it," says Matthew abruptly.

"No," gasps Bridie, grasping his arm. "No. I need you here with me."

"And I need you to live." He turns to her, his eyes glowing with love and anger in equal measure. "That man is the reason you're in this situation to begin with. The only reason you cast the curse is to protect yourself and the kids from him. After you told me, all I could think about is what he would've done to you if you hadn't cursed him. He brought his death upon himself. I won't let him bring it on you."

"No. That's not efficient," Tony states without an ounce of emotion. "It will take too long. We need to act immediately. I'll hire an assassin."

"A Shinobi?" I ask.

Tony looks me in the eye. "Yes."

I take a moment to delve into the Yang Pearl and allow its dragon energy to flow through me, cooling my emotions while sparking my intellect. Logically, hiring a Shinobi is the best choice. I give a single nod. Tony stands and heads out of the room, the phone already at his ear.

Auntie Cat watches him leave. Is she thinking about her brother and how she's going to help use Bridie's curse to kill him?

"Do you think your father meant for you to keep the Yang Pearl?" I ask her.

She looks startled for a moment, before her face creases with her thoughtful frown. "I don't know. He was drunk and held in the thrall of a spell that was slowly killing him. My father…" She pauses and clears her throat as she ducks her head. "You would've liked him. He was a rebel. If he hadn't been the Dragon Son, he would've walked the Wayward Way. He liked disruption and chaos, but he was all about honor. Mike never understood what that meant, at least not when he was young. I think Dad knew what Mike was up to with Sylvia, but he was so disgusted with both his sons, he didn't care. So, if he could, yes, I think he would've made me his heir." She gives a dry laugh. "Not that the clan would've allowed that."

I am like my grandfather because I don't much care about what the clan allows. Too bad I never got to meet him.

"I'll go with you when you go after George," says Matthew. "The energy of the Yin Pearl still resides within me. I can share that with Penny."

Bridie's eyes widen, and she sucks in a gasp. Before she can voice her protest, Penny speaks up. "Actually, Ba, that's the reason we need you here with Mum. A curse is different from a disease. We don't know if there'll be any effect on her when we cast it into George. You might need to use your healing powers on her."

Her mother shoots her a look of gratitude, though her father looks frustrated at the thought of being left behind.

"I also think Kai needs to be with you for moral support," Penny continues. "It's wrong not to let him know what's going on. We need to stop with the secrets, yeah?"

Bridie's face slides again into distress. "No. It's too much. I can't bear to have him with me while my soul is ripped to shreds."

"That's not what's going to happen…"

"Shush," Matthew says to her before taking Bridie into his arms. "Your mum doesn't want your brother there. Period."

And now I see what Penny had complained about, that her fathers had raised her to be strong while protecting Bridie from all the evils of the world. I need to stop seeing her family as perfect. They've got their share of dysfunction, with somewhat less murder.

Speaking of which, Tony reenters the kitchen, but remains standing. There's a bemused frown on his face, which is weird. He's seldom perplexed by anything. "I spoke to the chief of the Las Vegas Shinobi."

"Okay, and? What?" I ask. "Did he refuse the job?"

"Yes, but only because somebody already hired them to kill Kingfisher."

It's almost funny how everyone's faces go blank. Then Bridie breaks the shocked silence. "It's the curse. Death stalks him. Whoever wants him dead will act now."

That must be a pretty long list, and apparently we're not at the top. "Any idea who put out the hit?" I ask.

Tony shakes his head. "He wouldn't tell me, of course, but he did offer, for a price, to livestream the hit and allow us to watch. It happens tomorrow at one p.m."

"Did you agree?"

"I await your approval, Dragon Son."

It's so hard not to roll my eyes because he's so determined to show he's not in command. "You have it. Let's get this done."

Tony walks away again, phone to his ear. Everyone else at the table plans and debates our next moves, except me. I'm staring at Auntie Cat. Her father was right. His sons were bullshit. She should've been the Dragon Daughter. Everything would've turned out so much better. When this is all finished, and if we come out alive, I'm going to give the Yang Pearl to her.

Lennon

It's D-day and everyone's acting like nothing's wrong, aside from Uncle George wanting to murder us all and start a new family. At lunch, the adults talk about the earthquake like it's the most important thing going on. Aaron and Kai pick at their food in silence. They must sense something big is about to happen. That or they're bored. I mean, I'm picking at my food and not talking, either.

Conversation trickles down to an awkward hush. Spoons scrape bowls.

Bridie lifts a spoonful of jook. "I say, this porridge is quite nice. You must give me the recipe, May."

Really? We're going there? I mean, May's jook is bomb, but better than the truth? I don't think so.

The boys nudge each other while May recites the ingredients. When she's done, Aaron sets down his spoon and clears his throat. Then he glances at Tony and his face goes blank.

Kai glances at him and sighs. He takes a sip of tea, licks his lips, and speaks. "Um, I got something to tell everyone. Cuz everything's bad and if anything happens, I want everyone to know who I really am."

Jook sticks in my throat as I swallow too fast. Oh, hell no. Not that truth. Worst timing ever. Penny stiffens beside me before a soft, "Shite," escapes her lips.

Kai takes a deep breath. "I'm bi. Bisexual. I've known for a while. There just... there hasn't been a right time to say it and... um... yeah."

Aaron freezes, his gaze fixed on the kitchen wall behind Uncle Roy and Auntie Cat. The rest of my family goes poker-faced.

Bridie presses her hands to her heart as she gasps, "Oh, son, I'm so glad you told us. You know you can tell us anything, yeah? Ah," Tears fill her eyes. "I wish Gerry was here."

Matthew stands and embraces his son. "Thank you for telling us. I'm so proud of you."

I exhale a little. Okay, if it's just Kai, that's fine. The Sparrows are Wayward Way and everyone knows it. Tony watches with narrow eyes and a frown, but no outrage. This isn't his brother, so...

"I'm gay," Aaron blurts out.

And there it is.

Everyone looks at him before turning to Tony, who blinks once, twice, three times. I've never seen him blink so many times, not even when he found out about his mother. How can this be worse than that?

Kai pulls from his father's embrace and stands behind his friend. "So, we're not a thing, y'know, like, together. We're just friends who are, y'know, gay. It's just something we realized and thought our families should know."

Aaron stares at Big Brother, wide-eyed, not breathing. He, too, must notice the tight pull of Tony's lips.

Auntie Cat squares her shoulders and attempts a smile. "Well, I'm glad you told us. We can talk about it perhaps another time..."

"No." The word drops like a bomb. The explosion is in

Tony's eyes. "I won't stand for this nonsense. It's too much. I should have been stricter with you. Much stricter. Instead, I let you run wild with that boy and his family, who have already ruined Paul."

Kai shoots me and Penny a 'told you so' look.

"After all this is done, I'm taking you out of that school. You're not to see or speak to Kai or his family again."

Aaron's face reddens as he listens to Tony's rant. "What? You think that's gonna make me un-gay?"

"You are not gay." He says the word as if it's beneath contempt. "How can you be gay? I didn't raise you to be a homosexual. Not like them." He gives a scornful nod toward Kai's parents.

What the hell? This is way worse than I imagined. I thought Tony would be upset with Aaron for coming out because he doesn't like anyone being out about anything. This is different. This is hateful.

I glare at him. "Look, if Aaron says he's gay, he's gay. I'm cool with it and you should be, too."

"Do you think I care about being cool? I care about the two of you not disgracing me. I won't allow this. He will not be gay, and you will not carry on with that girl and her family any longer."

"I don't care about disgracing you," shouts Aaron. "I told Dad, and he didn't act like you. He accepted me."

Tony turns his fury back on him. "You told your father? When?"

"A couple of months ago, before he got all evil, and he was fine with it. He said he was proud of me."

"Of course he did," Tony's features twist with scorn. "He wants to get rid of you, you little fool. Now that he knows you're gay, he'll use it against you. You played right into his hands. You'll ruin us all with your foolishness."

"What are you talking about?" I yell at him.

"I'm talking about the clan turning against us because he's not normal."

My mouth drops open. "He is normal. There's nothing wrong with being gay."

"Forget it," snaps Aaron. "I knew he wouldn't listen. That he'd make a big deal out of it and blame someone else." The anger in his eyes burns as cold as his brother's. "This isn't about Dad. It's about me being gay and you not accepting it, because you can't, because you're so righteous, like there's anything righteous about being homophobic. There's not. You're a bigot."

He launches out of the room and Kai runs after him. Silence fills the room, thick as the porridge we just ate. What the hell just happened? I mean, when I told Aaron to be truthful with our family, I didn't think it would turn out like this.

Matthew glares at Tony. "You cocked that up, mate. I won't have you talk to my son like that."

"I didn't speak to your son," Tony replies coldly.

"No, you spoke at him," says Bridie. "As if he's somehow to blame."

"He is. I won't have him and Aaron bring dishonor to our clan."

"Bollocks." Matthew sneers. "You sound like my parents. I'm glad I left the Two Dragon Clan, so my son won't be subjected to that shit."

"Your son and my brother walk two different paths."

"Do they?"

"My brother will walk the path of honor and he will not be gay."

I press my thumb to my chest. "Hey, I'm the Dragon Son. And from now on, being gay in the clan is cool. That's my decree and everyone's gotta follow it, even you. Especially you."

We stare at each other, a hateful current of electricity crackling between us. I'm not afraid of him. I've got the Yang Pearl and could blast him out of the building if I wanted, and he knows it. What's he gonna do? Demand to be the Dragon Son after all? Too fucking bad. That boat sailed.

Penny stands and turns toward Tony like she's going to make a speech. Instead, she closes her eyes. I sense the Yin Pearl's power flowing toward him. His face goes blank as he freezes. I tap into my dragon power to see what she sees. A dark red aura swirls around Tony like a tornado. Penny aims her healing energy into its midst. A razor of resistance strikes like lightning, and she winces in pain. Then she reaches into the pinprick of power in her chest and sends a fiery burst of dragon energy into the aura. It disperses as if made of dust.

Tony gasps and grasps the edge of the table.

"Was that…" I ask.

"George," Penny replies. "He planted something in Tony, like a landmine." She turns to my brother. "Are you all right? I'm sorry I didn't act sooner. It took me a few minutes to figure out what was going on."

He places his hand over his mouth as if he's going to be sick. "My father… I mean, the Traitor… I remember now. The last time I saw him, here in the *kongsi*, he told me that Aaron is gay. He said that when I find out, I won't like it. I won't accept him. He told me to say things that will turn Aaron against me." He shakes his head. "I don't care if Aaron's gay. I want him to be safe and happy. I promised Mother that I'd take care of him, that I wouldn't let his father hurt him, and he used me to hurt him in the worst way." He bows his head.

Everyone in the room exhales. May stands and embraces her husband from behind. Cat reaches for his hand and squeezes. Roy's hands clench into fists, as if he's imagining what he'd like to do to Uncle George right now. Bridie and Matthew's outraged expressions soften with sympathy.

I sink back in my chair. I was so ready to blast him,

thinking the worst of him. It could've ruined everything. Uncle George must've known he'd need to stir the shit among us and what better weapon than Aaron to tear us apart? I turn to Penny and manage a smile. "You're fucking amazing, you know that?"

She gives a tight shrug. "I don't know about that. I think I just let George Lau know we're here."

Tony lifts his head and grimly nods. "Was anything else planted in me?"

Her brow wrinkles. "No. To be honest, I'm surprised that's all there was. He could've done a lot more damage through you."

"I wasn't alone with him for long. I remember now that Lennon arrived, and the Traitor said we'd continue our conversation later."

"He was alone with me." She grimaces at the memory. "I used Charm to fight him off. Was he alone with anyone else?"

Cat, Roy, and May all shake their heads, but would they remember if they had been? Tony didn't.

But I do. "I was alone with him and Head Elder. You better check me."

"Pretty sure I would've sensed it before now, but..." I feel the energy of the Yin Pearl flow around. She shakes her head as it withdraws. "No, you're good."

What would've happened if Uncle George had had more time with all of us? Had that been his plan all along, to turn us into puppets, fighting amongst each other? He'd come to the *kongsi* unannounced and short of time, expecting to win. He still expects to win, and maybe that's the weakness we should exploit.

"You should check everyone in the building," Tony says to Penny.

I glace at the kitchen clock. It's 12:45. "There's no time and it'll drain too much of her *chi.*"

Penny nods. "It has to wait until after we remove the curse from my mother."

Tony looks at the clock as well. Air hisses from his teeth. He says softly, "I have to apologize to Aaron."

May squeezes his shoulders before stepping away. "I'll have them help me take lunch up to the guards and keep them on the roof until you're done. Then you can tell him."

After she leaves, I say to Tony, "Don't let this play with your mind. That's why Uncle George did it. Don't let him win."

Big Brother doesn't reply. He stares at his lap, self-disgust clear on his face. Roy stands and taps him on the shoulder before nodding for him to follow. Me, he won't listen to, but he might take heed of another strong, silent masculine type, so it's all good. I reach out to the only person who listens to me.

You okay? Did that drain your energy?

She shrugs. *Not really. Not the part I need to heal Bridie, so it's fine.*

Are you ready for this?

No. You?

No.

We look in each other's eyes because we know, ready or not, here we go.

Penny

In the parlor, I direct Bridie to the love seat while Lennon and I position ourselves behind her. Matthew sits beside her, holding her hand. "Ba, no. Mum has to do this alone. We can't have your energy interfere with hers."

Bridie squeezes his hand as if she won't let go. He kisses her lips and caresses her cheek before whispering, "Good luck."

With a soft sigh, she lets go as he stands.

Lennon and I can't kiss for good luck or any reason. All we can do is exchange glances, nods, and Silent Speech.

We got this, he says.

We totally do. I know we do. That doesn't diminish the sick feeling in the pit of my stomach.

Cat and Roy take their places, blocking the two doors leading into the room. Tony syncs his phone to the television mounted above the mantle. A row of slot machines appears on the screen, their digital whirring and clinking echo off the dull gold walls of the casino. Garish colors whirl across the faces of the punters planted in front of each machine. I immediately recognize the two closest to the camera, Kingfisher and his son, Mikey-Boy.

I suck in my breath at the sight of them, thinking of the peril we'd so narrowly escaped. Kingfisher had claimed Bridie for himself and planned to give me to Mikey-Boy. We'd fought back and won with Lennon's help. I last saw Kingfisher frozen in place thanks to Lennon's use of *dim mak,* making him ripe for the curse Bridie placed on him. He looks no different with his shaved head, beady eyes, and tight Raiders jacket barely containing his wide frame.

Mikey-Boy appears almost military with his buzz-cut and camouflage hoodie. I wonder if he's still boxing until I notice the purple bruise beneath his left eye. Then again, Kingfisher could've punched him. From my brief conversation with him, he seemed trapped by his father and locked into doing whatever Kingfisher willed of him.

Bridie cringes at the sight of Kingfisher, and then winces as she notices Mikey-Boy. She turns to Tony. "That's his son with him. Can we... can we stop them? I don't think his son should have to watch him die."

Tony shakes his head. "This isn't our contract. We have no control over what happens."

"I don't want to watch." She turns away, her hands knit into a tight ball on her lap.

I do. Time for that blighter to pay the devil his due for all the misery he's caused.

As Kingfisher and his son continue playing the slots, I wonder why the Shinobi decided to kill him in public, in the middle of the day, in the middle of a casino. There can't be an easy escape route. Mikey-Boy keeps glancing over his shoulder until a cocktail server in high heels and a tight gold dress arrives, carrying a drink tray. He nudges his father, who turns from the slot machine long enough to snatch his beer from her hand, but not offer thanks. Mikey-Boy smiles and gives her a tip. They exchange a quick glance before she saunters away, her long black hair swaying against her back.

"Shite!" I exclaim.

"You think?" asks Lennon. He turns to Tony. "Is she Shinobi?"

Tony doesn't reply, his thousand mile stare fixed on the screen.

"Mikey-Boy hates his father," I say. "He blames him for his mother's death. He told me so himself."

The son's smile lingers as he watches his father suck down his beer. Mid-glug, Kingfisher freezes. Then he gives a violent cough, spewing suds all over the shiny face of the whirling slots. The bottle slips from his grasp, falling to the carpeted floor with a single bounce before rolling away. He grasps his throat, turning to his smiling son. Their eyes lock. Then King-fisher slumps forward, his face pressed against the screen, his girth holding him in place between the stool and the slot machine.

Tony switches off the TV as Lennon and I turn to Bridie. She's still turned away.

"Is he…" she whispers.

"Mum, it's time," I reply softly. I lean over and untangle her fingers, resting her hands on her thighs. "Close your eyes and breathe."

I raise my hand, and Lennon presses his palm against mine until I feel a light pressure. Then we lay our hands on Bridie's shoulders. I close my eyes and sink into the Yin Pearl, following its power as it flows through me, into Lennon, mingling with the energy of the Yang Pearl. We become one. I feel his guilt. He feels my grief. Neither of us is as confident as we try to appear. We're terrified of losing each other. All our weaknesses holding us back, keeping us safe from what? From this. Our destiny. Whatever happens next is all about us. With a mutual breath, our energy flows into Bridie. She gasps from pain or fear, I don't know and can't stop to comfort her.

The curse spreads through her with a rapid, rabid intelligence, staining her soul and laying her bare to disease and misfortune. It knows her heart of darkness and her greatest treasure. Its tendrils slide up her esophagus, wrapping around her larynx… No! We seize the curse at its root, like a weed, and tug. Bridie cries out in pain. I steel myself against soothing her and press on. The tendrils tighten their grasp. We send a bolt of energy through its core, shocking the curse until it loosens its grip. Then, like a vacuum, we suck the curse into the midst of the Yin Pearl. But it's not alone—it has taken a piece of my mother.

My eyes pop open. My hand, which started out flat-palmed, is now clenched with Lennon's. We exchange looks and I know he felt what happened. I let go of him to squeeze Bridie's shoulders.

"Mum?"

She doesn't reply, her fingers kneading that part of her chest where the curse took root. Her skin has lost all color.

Matthew joins her on the couch. "Bridie, love, are you all right?"

She shakes her head slowly as her hand slides to her throat. Her eyes are like wet emeralds as she croaks, "My voice. Ruined. I can't sing."

Her greatest treasure, gone, or rather devoured by the curse that wouldn't let go without taking its due. I sag as my knees buckle. Lennon wraps his arm around my waist and helps me to the couch. Bridie's blank stare slices me like a razor. She'd had the exact same expression when we'd heard Gerry and Matthew had been killed. When the shock wears off, she'll rage and weep, but for now, she mourns in silence.

"What happened?" asks Cat. "Didn't it work?"

"It did." Lennon answers. "But the curse took a part of Bridie's soul. The part that sings."

She gasps. "Is there anything we can do?"

I shake my head. "The curse devoured it."

Two tears roll down Bridie's cheeks, though her expression doesn't change.

Tony joins us, his stern expression easing as he gazes down on her. "I'm sorry. May is an amazing doctor. Perhaps she can help."

Bridie shakes her head, her voice like wet gravel. "No. Nothing can help. It's gone."

Matthew gathers her into his embrace. I can see the torment in his eyes. He blames himself, that he listened to his parents and agreed to steal the pearls. If he hadn't, none of this would've happened, but how could he know? Fault is a many-layered thing and when we peel this back to its core, we find George Lau.

I turn to Tony. "When do we strike the Traitor?"

Steel sparks in his eyes and something else: approval. "When can you be ready?"

I turn to Lennon. "What do you think? An hour?"

He nods. "Yeah. Maybe less, but let's take the full hour so…"

The door bursts open and two guards come rushing in, guns drawn. Everyone jumps to their feet. My heart pounds. George must've struck the first blow, which means he knows Lennon and I are here.

One guard speaks rapidly in Cantonese. Tony freezes, as if stunned. Lennon gives an anguished cry and hurries to his side. Cat covers her mouth like she's going to be ill, while Roy questions the guard in an angry tone. Oh, no! Did something happen to May?

Matthew pushes through them, standing in front of the guards while pounding his fist and shouting.

Not May.

I reach for Bridie and she grasps my hands in a death grip.

Tony snaps out of his daze. He taps his phone until it syncs with the TV. Security footage of the roof appears on the screen. The time stamp shows this happened several minutes ago. A guard aims an air rifle and fires at a drone. Kai and Aaron cheer him on while jeering at the drone and flipping it off.

Two black-clad men appear, grab hold of each boy, and vanish.

Bridie faints.

I catch hold of her and lower her onto the couch. Then I kneel beside her, stroking her face, and whispering, "It's all right. It's all right. We'll get them back, I promise."

I don't know how, but we will.

Penny

Placing my hand on Bridie's shoulder, I take a deep breath, tapping into the power of the Yin Pearl. I exhale and healing energy flows through me into her, soothing her fears and enhancing her courage. Her eyelids flutter open and she sits up, but she doesn't weep or wail. Matthew sits beside her, hunched over as if in deep pain, digging his fists into his temples. Bridie puts her arm around him and soothes him as he soothed her only moments ago.

I stand and stare at them, thinking of all we've suffered. This ends now. The Yin Pearl heals, but it also destroys, and I'm in the mood for destruction.

Lennon is standing in a tight circle with his family, but he joins me when I catch his eye.

"What's the plan?" I ask.

"We wait for Uncle George to contact us. Obviously, he wants to exchange the pearls for their lives."

"Aaron might be safe, but he'll kill Kai once he has the pearls."

He gives a grim nod. "I know. Auntie Cat says she'll negotiate with him, but I don't think she has much sway."

"We have to go to the Eighty-eight and cast the curse into the manky bastard. That'll give us something to negotiate with."

"I agree, but," he sighs, "how do you feel?"

Why lie? The stress of the kidnapping has further depleted me. "Like shite."

"Same. Auntie Cat can at least stall for time while she negotiates."

"True." What else can we do?

We settle on the love seat. Lennon closes his eyes, resting his hands on his thighs, his thumb touching his middle finger. I do the same, but with flat palms and slow breath, concentrating on the pinprick of power that still contains dragon fire. It spreads through me, warming the chill of fear and evaporating the fog of despair. Tony's voice interrupts the flow of strength returning to my limbs.

"He sent me a text."

A wave of dizziness hits me as I open my eyes too quickly, followed by nausea as I see the text displayed on the TV screen. It's a photo of Kai and Aaron standing on either side of George Lau. Both boys look dazed and placid, as if unaware of the terrible danger they're in. George smiles, his eyes bright, like a dad posing for a selfie with his son.

Beneath the photo is a two word text.

Call me.

Bridie stands and rasps out, "Give him whatever he wants. Those pearls aren't worth our boys' lives. You give him what he wants. You understand me?" Her last words are a muffled shriek.

Matthew stands and takes her in his arms. We exchange glances and he nods.

"We'll get him back," I say.

"I know. Don't lose yourself. You're just as valuable to us as him."

I know that, but it lifts my spirits to hear it.

We wait until he leads her out of the room, then Cat speaks. "I'll talk to him."

"How will you keep him from controlling you?" asks Tony.

"We'll put him on speaker."

"So he can control us all?"

While they debate, I tap into the Yin Pearl, thinking of how I used its power to shield us from bullets in London. "I can stop him from controlling us."

They stare at me, frowning, skeptical, because they haven't seen me rock 'n roll.

"Are you sure?" asks Cat.

I nod. "The Yin Pearl does more than heal. It shields as well."

"She can totally do it," adds Lennon. "You won't believe all the things she can do."

Doubt fades from their expressions, but their frowns remain. I understand. I'm not a member of their clan, and I'm using one of their most powerful weapons. It can't be easy to swallow, even with so much at stake. There's no time to soothe their wounded pride. I hold out my hand. Tony gives me his phone. It's heavy, with a case that can probably stop bullets, like you'd expect from him.

"Need a boost?" asks Lennon.

"Sure. Why not?"

We exchange quick smiles as our palms touch. His *chi* surges through me, empowering me further. I tap the number on the screen. Then I gather his power and mine and form a filter around the phone that will allow sound out but contain all other energy.

George answers with a command, "Bring me the pearls now."

His will pushes at the barrier of the filter, attempting to find a slit of weakness to ram through. Lennon and I keep it sealed tight against the growing onslaught of the Wisdom Pearl. I feel his presence, almost as if he's beside us, looking us up and down and considering our strength. After a few tense moments, his will subsides like the tide drawing back as a larger wave approaches.

He speaks again, this time with an amused purr. "So, nephew, you've become a man. Wait until the clan learns you fucked a gypsy so you could use the pearls."

Don't let him get to you, I say to Lennon.

He mentally scoffs. *He can pound sand.*

"What do you want?" Tony asks, his voice and face devoid of expression.

"Ah, my erstwhile son. You know what I want. Give me the pearls or I'll kill your brother and his friend."

"You'd kill your own son?"

"He's not my son, any more than you. I did a DNA test after he was born, of course. He's mine by blood, but he's his mother's son. She turned him against me. He chose you over me. I choose the pearls over him."

"George," says Cat, sharply. "You can't kill your son."

"Ah, Cat." He chuckles. "I killed your mother. I killed our brother. Why wouldn't I kill my son?"

"You didn't kill my mother."

"Not directly, but you blame me for her death. As for Mike, the Shinobi held him while I pulled the trigger. It was my pleasure to kill the man who took everything from me. Now, I have it all. Everything he had and more, except the last two pearls. They are mine, my birthright, as the true Dragon Son."

"Why should we give them to you? Why should we trust you won't kill the boys, anyway?"

"You want those boys to live? You'll do what I say. I want my nephew and his girlfriend to bring me the pearls. They'll show me how to use them. Then I will release them, along with my son and his friend, unharmed. On my honor. I'll make this easy. You have until four o'clock to bring me the pearls. If not, I'll kill them and live-stream their deaths so you can watch."

"I want to come with Lennon and Penny and stay with them, to make sure you keep your end of the deal, and I want Roy with me."

"I heard you two were back together. Congratulations."

Her careful facade slips as her eyes flash with anger. "Stop it."

"Mike ruined your life, the same way he tried to ruin mine. Why are you defending his sons?"

George's will intensifies, straining against the barrier, trying to reach Cat. It feels like I've trapped a nest of angry hornets under a box and they're stinging through the cardboard. Lennon boosts his energy flow, which keeps the box contained, but at the cost of our internal strength. They need to end the call now.

"Do we have a deal?" asks Cat.

"Bring whoever you want, Cat. Bring the whole family. Be here at four." George hangs up.

As Lennon's energy recedes, the phone drops from my numb hand. He and I drop to the couch. I close my eyes and pant rather than breathe. I'm done and so is he. It will take days, not hours, to restore our *chi* to a level sufficient to take on our enemy. As the buzzing in my ears diminishes, I hear the others discussing our plight.

"If we give them our energy now, we might not have enough to empower them to cast the curse into George," says Roy.

"Is there anyone else in the *kongsi* who we can trust to share their chi?" asks Cat.

"Yes," Tony replies. "Me."

"You can't. We need you strong enough to join forces with Jeremiah Walks Long and take over the Eighty-Eight."

"I can do it," says Matthew.

My eyelids flutter open. I didn't realize he'd returned. I want to protest that Bridie needs him, but I know he'll argue that she needs her children alive even more. He looks different, stronger, no longer bewildered from being trapped in his own mind for all those years.

"It wasn't just the Yin Pearl that kept me alive for two years. It was Jade Dragon. I don't know why he did. Maybe he knew this day would come. I still feel his power within me."

He sits between me and Lennon and lays his hands on our shoulders. I'm too weak to do more than close my eyes. My shoulder tingles as his *chi* moves through me like a slow, electric shock. As it reaches the Yin Pearl, his energy unblocks its flow. Healing pours out of it, through Matthew, and into Lennon. Then I sense the gold thread of Jade Dragon that connects all three of us. It becomes a live wire, making that pinprick in my chest burn like coal as its energy flows through us, strengthening us all.

Matthew's hand slips away. I exhale, expelling the last of the toxins that had blocked my flow of chi. I feel amazing. Better than I had before we healed Bridie. Lennon is sitting up straight, eyes no longer dull, and the color returned to his face. I examine my father with worried eyes, but he also appears energized rather than drained. Maybe he's right. Maybe Jade Dragon stored a reserve of power within him for such a day, but why? Is it even worth wondering? That dragon will never tell us.

We stand, and Lennon draws me into his embrace. We're way past the approval of our relatives. What we do next, we do together, as one. Life and death, it all comes down to us.

The one thing we didn't expect? Traffic. George wasn't being generous when he gave us until four to reach the Eighty-Eight. Road closures around the Titanic have made for a rush hour snarl of epic proportion. What should've been a ten-minute drive has taken almost an hour and we're still more than a block from our destination. Roy's attempt to maneuver through the side streets has landed us in a one-way alley, creeping forward every few minutes.

The Eighty-Eight looms ahead, the dragon gate forming a square hole above its center, surrounded by clouds reflecting off its sharp glass surface. I stare at it through the sunroof of our SUV, thinking about Kai being held prisoner there, George feeding him and Aaron lies, turning them against us, while pumping them for information.

"This blows," says Lennon. "We won't get there in time. We have to walk."

"If we walk, they'll follow us," says Roy.

"You don't think they're following us right now?"

"Of course they are. But if we walk, we won't have the protection of the car when we empower you to cast the curse."

"If we use Swift Steps, they won't be able to follow. What do you think, Auntie Cat?"

She stares out the front passenger window without saying a word. She's been silent since we got in the car. None of us have thought about how difficult this might be for her. We're about to cast a deadly curse into her brother. I don't know how far gone Kai would have to be for me to do that. I guess as far as George, which I can't imagine happening.

Since she doesn't answer, I bring up a point. "Won't that drain our energy?"

"Yeah." Lennon draws out the word. "But not much. We don't have to go far."

"How close do you have to be?" asks Cat, looking as if she's awoken from an uneasy dream.

"Closer than this," I reply.

"How about the end of the street?"

I peer through the front window. That would put us directly across the street from the Eighty-Eight. We'd planned to park in the delivery zone behind the building before putting our plan into action, but this might be better than suspiciously lingering inside the car.

"It could work, except Roy has to drive and can't channel his energy into us."

He lifts his hands from the wheel. "We're moving so slowly, if I put it in park for a few minutes, no one will notice."

"I know George," says Cat. "He knows we're stuck in traffic and he's enjoying it. He wants us to squirm and become frantic so we'll make mistakes. Let him go on believing that's what's happening."

I shudder as a chill moves through me. Kai would never do anything like this to me, but who knows what George has done to his mind by now? My heart pounds and I suppress a desire to throw open the door and run to the building to save him. Cat is right. George knows what he's doing.

Lennon takes my hand. His squeeze tells me that what I'm feeling for Kai, he's feeling for Aaron. I close my eyes and start taking slow, even breaths. I feel him do the same. Our minds brush and connect, but we don't speak. We feel the fear, hate, and doubt poisoning our confidence in ourselves and each other. After another breath, we concentrate on the pinprick of dragon power in our chests. We allow its fire to spread, burning away the negative energy, allowing the power of our pearls to flow more freely through us. That's when we sense it.

The Wisdom Pearl.

It swirls with a vitality that seeks and gains. Restless, hungry for the knowledge that enables survival, and full of persuasion that extracts what it wants from the world.

Persuasion, coming at us full force, filtered through the Summoning Pearl, drawing us to him.

He's here. George Lau. In the car, surrounding me and Lennon with his whispers.

Let go.

Give in.

Be mine.

All will be well.

All you have to do is surrender.

I ignore his voice and concentrate on its source of power. The Wisdom Pearl. The Summoning Pearl. They wield a different type of energy, one that I recognize because I've brushed against it several times. Red and green. Fire and water. Ebb and flow. It's an energy that smolders before it burns and holds a deep grudge. A power that waits, and wants, and devours.

Do you feel that? I ask Lennon.

Yeah.

We don't have to say, because we know. That energy, those pearls, they're not from Jade Dragon. They're from Master Stoorworm.

I feel them, both dragons, somewhere nearby, small as birds, huge as airplanes, watching, waiting to see which of their descendants prevail.

Lennon squeezes my hand so hard it hurts. I squeeze back with equal strength. The pain sharpens our minds. We delve into our pearls and create a barrier against George's onslaught. He doesn't back down. The whispers continue, accompanied by mental images.

Kai and Aaron splayed on the ground like dropped dolls covered in blood, bullet holes in their foreheads, their brains splattered on the wall behind them.

Tony, his hands bound behind his back, dragged onto a wooden stage in a courtyard that I somehow know is part of the clan's main compound in Hong Kong. A jeering crowd cheers as an executioner slits his throat from behind.

May, still pregnant, dragged onto that same stage, her feet slipping on her dead husband's blood. The executioner strangles her in front of that same crowd.

Bridie and Matthew startle awake in their dark bedroom as the door smashes open. Guns blaze and their bodies jerk as the bullets pierce their flesh.

This isn't real. He's not real. He's not here.

Except he is. And if he is, doesn't that mean I can strike back? Why go to him if he's already come to us? Can I? Should I? I don't want to waste my shot.

Go for it, comes Lennon's faint whisper. *I'll grab hold of him.*

It will take all our combined power. We can't break away to ask Cat and Roy for more. We have to do it now, while we still can.

Let's do it.

The energy of the Yang Pearl flows away from me and toward George. It winds around the energy of the Wisdom and Summoning Pearls, holding it in place. George turns his attention from me to throw all his energy at Lennon. The Yang

Pearl strains to contain his power. Within seconds, the bond breaks.

Within those seconds, I reach for the curse and send it past the pearls and into George's essence. It clings to its new host like a leech, sucking in, taking hold, eager to fulfill its deadly magic.

George retreats immediately, the energy of his pearls sucking him away as if through a vacuum.

I gasp as I open my eyes, pressing my fingers to the pinprick, which burns like a hot ember embedded under my skin. I'm too weak to lift my head, so I turn it slowly toward Lennon. He's doing the same, pressing the source of his dragon fire while staring at me, his dark eyes glowing with pride against his pale skin. We did it. We share a smile, our hands still clutched in a death grip. My fingers ache and I flex them to release the pressure.

"What happened?" asks Cat.

Lennon takes a couple of breaths before he can answer. "Uncle George. He attacked us. We fought him off. Penny cast the curse into him."

"Are you sure?"

I nod because I'm still not strong enough to speak.

She and Roy speak in excitable voices, but I don't hear what they say. I close my eyes, longing to drift off to sleep, but I can't. I cast the curse, but Kai and Aaron remain prisoners.

Lennon clasps my hand again. The warmth of Cat's *chi* flows through him to me. Nice, but not enough. Even as I think this, I feel something like a hook digging into the pinprick in my chest, connecting a wire of energy between the three of us. Cat gasps. A seed of power buried in her chest long ago bursts open, spreading dragon fire through her to us.

It burns.

Gloriously.

Dragon fire cascading through us.

Our energy becomes one flow, gaining strength and empowering our entire beings.

Cat draws away, reducing the flow until it ceases.

We all draw breath as one as we open our eyes.

"Jade Dragon?" Lennon asks his aunt.

She nods, her fingers kneading that spot in her sternum. "It must be from when I wore the Yang Pearl. I had no idea it was still there."

"What the hell is going on?" asks Roy.

Before any of us can answer, she pulls her buzzing phone from her pocket. Her brow furrows as she reads the screen. "Come now or I'll kill them."

My heart pounds. I swallow hard against the burn of panic in my throat. "Tell him you kill them, you die. I'm the only one who can remove the curse."

Cat taps the message on her screen. We wait. Then, her phone buzzes, and she reads, "Remove the curse and I'll release them."

"Standoff," Lennon spits out. "What do we do? Text back: we'll remove the curse when you release them?"

"No," says Roy, adamantly. "Don't keep playing his game. George is the king of backing his enemy into a corner. That's what he did to Mike when Mike wanted Tony to be the Dragon Son. George pretended to be on his side while luring him into a trap."

"This back and forth is pointless," says Cat. "I'll call him and negotiate our terms."

"You can't," I say. "That'll take too much of my energy."

She looks me in the eye. Her gaze has a glimmer of dragon fire. "I don't need you for this."

I nod. As the car slows to another stop, she opens the door and gets out.

Roy makes an exclamation of surprise. He puts the car in park and opens his door.

"Don't," says Lennon. "She can only hold him back for herself."

"How?" he demands, "If you don't help her."

"When we were sharing chi, it somehow activated the residue of Yang Pearl within her. And something happened…" My voice trails off because I don't know how to explain to Roy about the dragon fire. I turn to Lennon, pressing the pinprick spot on my chest.

"She has her own energy from Jade Dragon," he explains to Roy. "Enough to fight off Uncle George on her own."

Roy stares at us in this way that makes me think he's seeing himself and Cat at our age. And that didn't turn out well. "Are you absolutely sure?"

Neither Lennon nor I answer because we're not.

We look out the window at Cat, pacing on the sidewalk beside our SUV. Her head is ducked, and she's speaking intently. I think of how Tony radiated a dark red aura under George's control. I tap into the Yin Pearl to gaze at Cat through that same filter. A purple glow surrounds her, sparkling red and blue, like an opal.

"She's fighting him off," I say.

"Should we help her?" asks Lennon.

Before I can answer, Cat shoves her phone in her pocket and motions for us to join her. We wait for the SUV to stop before climbing out. Roy unrolls his window. By now, we're almost at the end of the alley.

Cat's eyes are clear and grim as she speaks, "George will meet us in the lobby with the boys." She turns to Roy. "Not you. Only me." He protests, and she speaks over him. "He'll release Aaron and Kai at that time. I'll take their place as hostage. Lennon and Penny will heal him and he'll release me. They'll give him their pearls in return for their freedom."

"Bullshit." Lennon crosses his arms and plants his feet.

"Agreed," says Roy. "After he gets the pearls, he'll kill them."

"Good luck with that, cuz I'm not giving that asshole the Yang Pearl."

Cat's face squeezes with impatience. "Of course not. First, we get the boys released, then we attack him." She turns to me. "You said the curse makes him vulnerable to anyone who wants to kill him?"

I nod.

"Did you give him your word of honor?" asks Roy quietly.

"Of course I did, and he gave me his. As if that's worth anything between us." Cat lays her hand on his arm. "Go to Tony and Jeremiah. Tell them to attack as soon as the boys are released."

They take a moment to look into each other's eyes. Finally, together and now one of her brothers is tearing them apart again. It has to stop. We'll make it stop.

Or die trying.

There's no stoplight at the end of the alley, but traffic on First Street is at a standstill across all four lanes. We weave around the cars, their rumbling engines providing pockets of warmth against the chill. When we reach the sidewalk, I crane my neck like a tourist and gawk at the Eighty-Eight. Sharp-edged, shiny, and full of evil. Why do we have to stop him? Why can't those damn dragons smash through their gate and send Uncle George tumbling down? Because they want to watch us suffer and strive. If we die, I guess they'll have fun watching Uncle George play with their pretty pearls. Fuckers.

"Where's the entrance?" asks Penny.

That's a good question. Like a lot of high-rises, the Eighty-Eight has businesses on the ground floor, including a bank and one of those places that make sushi burritos. A homeless couple and their dog squat in front of the restaurant, holding up their cardboard signs while begging for spange. The dog is a nice touch, making it less obvious they're with the Beggar Clan. A quick glance up and down the street reveals Beggars huddled in the nooks and crannies of the surrounding buildings. Jeremiah must be somewhere nearby, watching and hoping I live since my oath dies with me.

We hurry around the corner, passing another bank, until we reach a set of double-doors with the number 88 inscribed in the marble panel above them. The heavily tinted glass prevents us from seeing inside. We stop and wait, but no welcoming committee appears.

Auntie Cat stares at the number, her gaze unfocused, turning to me. "Whatever happens next, I want you to know that I love you and I only ever wanted what was best for you. I'm sorry I kept so many things hidden from you."

As she speaks, I think of the last time I saw my mom alive. She, too, hid so many things from me. I could sense it, and I was angry. I remember her watching me go into my bedroom, her eyes pleading for the words I was too tired and pissed off to say. "I love you, too."

A quick, sad smile lightens my aunt's face. Blink and it's gone, replaced by steel determination. She strides ahead to the doors.

Penny and I look at each other. No words. Our hands clasp like magnets, a surge of energy locking us in place. Whatever happens next is on us.

The doors swing open as we approach and we enter the lobby. Everything is gold-veined white marble, from the diamond-patterned floor, to the walls, to the reception desk. Our footsteps echo in the stony chill of this monument to capitalism.

"Maybe this is the wrong entrance," Penny says, glancing around.

"Maybe." I release her hand and go around the marble panel behind the desk. It leads to a pair of double doors. I try the handles, but they're locked. Should I try forcing them open? I don't want to use my energy for nothing.

A startled shriek splits the silence. Penny!

I dash around the panel and see Auntie Cat squeezing Penny in a chokehold. Penny claws at her arm while struggling for breath. Auntie Cat stares at me vacantly, as if I'm a stranger, not even flinching when armed men come striding out from behind the marble panel behind them. The long, cylindrical silencers attached to their weapons ensure no one outside will hear any carnage and call the police. One of them hands my aunt a gun, which she presses to Penny's temple. Penny stops struggling and closes her eyes, as if trying to contain her panic.

What do I do? Think quick. I mean, this is pointless, right? Uncle George needs Penny to heal him, so Auntie Cat won't hurt her or me. So why is he doing this? A display of power. He's showing me what he's capable of and using my emotions to throw me off my game. I can't let him do that.

"Are you all right?" I call out.

"Yeah," comes out as a croak. Penny's mind brushes against mine. *We shouldn't have let her talk to him. I really thought she could hold him off.*

I thought she could, too. He must've planted something in her, the way he did to Tony, so she didn't know until it triggered her.

Sounds right. Now what?

Good question.

I lift my shoulders in a tight shrug and ask aloud, "So, now what?"

An elevator door opens in the next corridor. Auntie Cat drags Penny inside. A goon motions with his gun for me to join them.

I stall for time with, "Where are you taking us?"

"To the Gold Dragon," the goon replies, his eyes as glazed as my aunt's.

My mouth drops open. No. Way. "Gold Dragon? Really?"

In Chinese legends, gold dragons are the most powerful, best, luckiest, you name it, of all dragons. It's also the color associated with the emperor. Calling yourself Gold Dragon is basically proclaiming yourself to be emperor. You gotta be tripping balls or on one hell of an ego trip, or both, to do that.

The goon motions again, and I allow myself to be hustled into the elevator by his squad. He presses the button for the 39th floor. As we head up, I reach out, brushing against Auntie Cat's mind, and find the solid wall of Uncle George's will. She maintains her death-grip on Penny, her soulless eyes not meeting my gaze. I could blast her with the Yang Pearl, but what if her finger slips on the trigger and she puts a bullet in Penny's head?

Penny's eyes meet mine in the reflection of the mirrored elevator door. Her jaw clenches tight with the effort to appear calm. Her mouth is closed and breath comes in spurts through her nose. She's terrified. Of course she is. I am, too.

Should we blast them, I ask her, *the way we did to Matthew's parents?*

No. We need to save our power to go up against George. Remember what Bridie said. As long as he has the curse within him, whoever wants him dead can kill him. I can't let anything happen to Kai. He has to go home alive to Bridie and Matthew.

Even if it kills her. I don't protest or say a contradictory word because I feel the same way about Aaron. If we both die saving them, so be it.

So be it. Determination glints in the reflection of her eyes. What is it about being here, in the clutches of our enemy, at the end of our lives, that makes me love her even more?

Don't give up yet, she says. *We'll have our shot. I didn't expect him to be so powerful. How is he keeping control of so many people without burning out?*

I don't know. He got ahold of the Wisdom Pearl's manual. Maybe there was something in there about that.

It must take some sort of toll on him. That's where we'll find his weakness.

And that's where we'll hit him.

As plans go, it's not the greatest, but it's all we've got. Plus, Uncle George knows my weaknesses. They'll be in the room with me. I glance back at Auntie Cat. When the time comes, will I be fighting her as well as Uncle George? I could never hurt her. He knows that. But what about him? The only person he's never threatened is her. Does he still feel guilty about her mother's death? Could she be his weakness as well?

The elevator door opens and the goon squad leads us along a short corridor to a thick glass door that swings open. They hustle us through the doorway and along a wood-paneled hallway into a huge open space. A wall of windows offers a panoramic view of the San Francisco Bay, from the Golden Gate to the Bay Bridge. Rows of men and women face the opposite wall, their heads bowed in reverence.

A dais stands against that wall with three stairs leading to an ornate platform with red and gold panels carved with fierce, twining dragons. At its center, Uncle George sits on a wide, low-backed, gold-embroidered couch with intricate lacquered wood carvings. It looks familiar…

No. Way.

I saw that same throne when my family visited the Forbidden City in Beijing.

Yeah.

Uncle George has made himself a replica of the Emperor's throne. He really is tripping balls, which makes him even more dangerous.

Aaron and Kai stand on either side of the stairs, their faces placid despite the guards pointing guns at them. Shit. I don't have a clue how we're going to get out of this. We can't risk their lives, but we can't let him have the pearls. What do we do?

Uncle George smiles as we approach his throne, beaming approval on his sister as if she'd done something cute. "Cat, you can let her go now."

Auntie Cat releases Penny, but remains directly behind her.

"More games, I see," he remarks, as if bored. As if he's already won. He looks at Penny. "What's this one called?"

She lifts her chin. "Strowler Death Curse."

"You will remove it."

"If you insist."

His smile becomes a sneer. "Do you really think I haven't considered that you'd kill me rather than heal me? My guards have orders to kill you all if I die. I planted this order within them, just as I did with Tony. My death won't stop them."

Of course he did. Shit. Is there any way to come out of this alive?

He spreads his hands, palms down, and inhales deeply, as if breathing in power. "This throne is directly above the center of the dragon gate. I built it to gather energy from any dragon that flies through. Two have done so and I have that energy here." He presses his fingers to his sternum. "You can't stop me." As he says those words, a wave of his will comes at us. Penny raises a shield of energy to protect us. He continues speaking, battering at the shield. "You will remove the curse and give me your pearls. Now."

I can feel Penny struggling to hold him back. I shout, "If you drain her *chi*, she can't heal you."

The onslaught stops. She teeters backward, pressing a hand to her chest. I clasp her other hand so I can share my *chi* with her.

Uncle George stands and motions to Aaron's guard. The guard clamps down on Aaron's shoulders, making him kneel. Then he presses the business end of his pistol's silencer into the base of Aaron's skull.

"You won't kill him," I say, trying to convince myself. "He's your son."

He gives a bitter chuckle. "I have no need for a faithless son compelled to obey me. I remarried and my wife is pregnant with twin boys. Boys who will be what Mike and I never were. Fate works in my favor now. I can start over and do everything right. I will abolish the Two Dragon Clan. The Gold Dragon Clan will take its place, and we will rule the Crossroads forever. My sons will be raised correctly, but they will never take my place. These pearls can unlock the power of immortality. I will live forever and rule as the Gold Dragon."

Tripping. Balls.

Pearl power is a hell of a drug and he's got the Wisdom and the Summoning Pearls fueling his delusions.

Can the pearls really make him immortal? asks Penny

I don't know, and I don't want to find out.

"You don't believe me." Uncle George says this like an accusation. "Just like your father. Always in my way, taking what's mine. My wife, my son, my birthright." His voice rises with each item on his list. Spittle flies from his mouth as he shouts, "Everything!"

He jabs a finger toward Aaron. "His life means nothing to me. Any sacrifice is acceptable to gain immortality and claim my birthright as the next dragon."

Penny takes a shaky breath before asking, "How do we know you won't kill him and the rest of us after we heal you?"

Uncle George smiles. "You don't. All you know is if you don't heal me, I will kill him. Then Kai. Then Cat. Then you. If I can't live, no one can."

He motions for a middle-aged woman in the front row to step forward. She climbs the stairs without hesitation, hands folded, head bowed as she comes to a stop before him. The placid sheen of her eyes doesn't change as he presses his hand against her chest.

"This is Leung Hoi-Yan, head of surveillance. Ah-Yan failed to inform me that you and your girlfriend had left London and arrived in San Francisco."

"Forgive me, Gold Dragon," the woman states, as if reciting a line.

Uncle George cocks an ear. "Who am I?"

"You are the Gold Dragon who lives for ten thousand years."

He nods his approval before his mouth pulls with fake regret. "You've been very useful, Ah-Yan, but you failed me, and there's only one penalty for that."

A hum of energy fills the air. Leung Hoi-Yan's eyes roll upward as her mouth drops open. Her body goes slack, head lolling and limbs dangling. She should've dropped to the floor, but she's held in place as if by a vacuum.

Uncle George appears to swell, his face reddening and his body becoming fuller, straining against the fabric of his clothes. His eyes remain open, lit with ecstasy, as if he's taking a hit off a powerful drug. His hand jerks several times as if pulling out whatever's left of her while chanting, "All mine. All mine. All that you had, all that you were, are now mine."

The hum ends abruptly. She drops backwards off the stairs, her skull making a sickening crack as it hits the floor, her splayed body lifeless. Two goons scuttle over to lift her body and carry it away. Uncle George shudders and shakes his limbs as his body returns to normal.

Penny presses her hands to her mouth to keep from screaming. I freeze, nausea and fear zigzagging through my body. What has he done? Is he some kind of fucking vampire, sucking up people's *chi* to empower himself? How do we fight against that?

I don't want to ask, but I need to know. "Is that what happened to Head Elder?"

"To him and his worthless son. Speaking of which," Uncle George motions for Aaron to join him.

"No," I shout. "Stop it, you sick fuck." I lunge toward him, and two goons grab hold of me.

He places a tender hand on his son's chest. "I don't hate you, but you're more useful to me dead than alive. You understand."

"Yes," Aaron responds with a docile gaze.

"Who am I?"

"The Gold Dragon who lives for ten thousand years."

"That's right. I won't forget you. I promise." Uncle George sighs before beginning his countdown. "Five, four, three…"

"Stop," I shout. "We'll do it."

He doesn't lower his hand. "Then do it. Now."

Penny swallows hard before speaking. "You need to be seated or you'll faint. I don't want your guards killing us because you fell."

Uncle George stares at her with narrow suspicion before turning to his sister. "Is that true?"

"Yes," Auntie Cat replies with no change in expression.

He motions for Aaron to return to Kai's side. Then he settles on his throne.

Kill him? asks Penny. *He'll kill us all, anyway.*

I suck in a shaky breath. So this is where it ends. I really didn't want Aaron and Kai to die, but we're all *Xia*, all warriors on the Crossroads. We're born to die in battle.

Let's do it.

I love you.

I feel that in every part of my body. If only we'd had more time. So many things I wanted to say and do. All I can do now is say, *I love you.*

We press our palms together and inhale as one.

Stop.

That faint voice. It's not me or Penny. It's Auntie Cat. *He doesn't have all of me. The power of the Yang Pearl still protects my core.*

I feel Penny's doubt and echo it with my own. *Why didn't you say something sooner?*

I couldn't. He was too focused on me. Now, he's focused on healing. I can act.

Act how?

Pour all your energy into me. I can attack him directly, through his own power.

Do we believe her? I ask Penny.

Do we have any choice? she replies.

She could stop us from killing him if she's still under his control.

I'm not, says the whisper. *Please, believe me.*

I want to, but how? Then I feel it, what was missing before while she was under his control. Her. Auntie Cat. Her love pours through our connection. She's always believed in me and supported me like no one else. But Uncle George knows that..

No time to question or debate. I have to trust that her love is stronger than his hate. I take a deep breath and channel my *chi* through my body and into my palm, where it joins Penny's *chi.* Our two streams of power become one and flow into Auntie Cat. All other feelings within me disappear. I'm one with them in the vortex of our power.

We stop fighting George's energy and allow it to surround us, gather it to us. We join his flow, sense his triumph as he thinks he has us all now. The power of the dragon gate joins our flow from him to us. We take that power and allow it to flow through us, into the Yin and Yang Pearls. Liquid lightning pulses in our chests. With a single thrust, we release it.

Energy explodes throughout the throne room and beyond, overpowering everyone in George's thrall, in San Francisco,

Hong Kong, London, anywhere he's wormed into someone's brain. We see and feel them, all of them, covering their ears and grimacing as his hold on them is ripped away. The minions standing before us fall to the ground unconscious. All but Aaron and Kai, who we shelter from our storm.

We open our eyes. George quivers on his imperial throne, eyes closed as he takes deep breaths, trying to reclaim the power of his pearls. Too late. We're already there, inside the flow of the Wisdom and Summoning Pearls, feeling his feeble attempt to summon us to him and control our will. We delve into him, seeking the blood curse that demands its due, and find it wrapping its tendrils around his heart.

His greatest fear is that he'll die like his mother.

We take hold of that evil magic, as we had with his mother, and squeeze.

George clutches his chest, his mouth gaping open, a raspy rattle coming from his throat as he realizes he can't breathe. He swivels toward his son and gestures frantically for help.

Aaron's face is Tony-cold. He blinks once before turning away. Kai joins him, putting his arm across his shoulders.

"George," the Cat part of us says aloud.

He turns to her, eyes bulging, drool foaming from his gurgling mouth.

"I killed your mother. I thought you should know."

Fury overcomes the fear in George's eyes. Using his remaining strength, he stands, stretching out his arms, attempting to throw what's left of his power at her, a weak burst of energy we easily deflect.

"This is for my mother," says the Cat part of us. "I do blame you for her death."

George's limbs jerk as we squeeze the life out of him. He crumples like a broken puppet, falling down the stairs and landing at our feet.

Dead.

Our streams of energy separate, flowing back within each of us.

I am myself again, staring at my uncle's corpse. I guess I should feel something, like, I don't know? Happy? He killed my dad, and before that, he set up Dad to kill Gerry and Matthew. So much destruction, all so he could be Gold Dragon, or immortal, or whatever the hell else he was trying to be. I'm torn between wanting to kick the shit out of his body and just walking away.

"Is he dead?" asks Aaron, his back still turned.

"Pretty sure," I reply.

Auntie Cat, Penny, and I all exchange glances. We felt him die, but is that good enough?

"Don't turn around," says our aunt as she aims a gun at her brother's head. It's got a silencer, but that won't make this any nicer.

"Wait," says Penny.

She kneels beside Uncle George, grimacing as she loosens his tie enough to unbutton his collar. Then, reaching around his neck, she tugs on a thick gold chain until she yanks an oblong pendant out from under his shirt and over his head. She stands, dangling the chain between her fingers. It has four settings. The top one holds the Wisdom Pearl, its jade green streaked with blood red veins, the bottom one holds the Summoning Pearl, shimmering opalescent in the light, and two empty settings in-between, obviously reserved for the Yin and Yang Pearls.

Just looking at the other pearls sharpens the pinprick in my chest. Penny must feel it, too, since she shoves the pendant into her coat pocket and zips it closed.

Auntie Cat leans over, holding the gun to her brother's temple. Her arm jerks back with the muffled blast. I look away because I don't want to watch his head explode.

"You okay?" whispers Penny, who's also turned away.

"Yeah." I pause. "Do you feel…"

"Kind of weirdly great? Yeah."

That's a good way to describe this feeling. Instead of being totally drained, the power of the dragons courses through my veins. I'd feel like I was on top of the world if it weren't for my messed up family. It's just like in London when Jade Dragon's power kept us going for days.

Maybe those dragons are on our side after all.

Now there's a funny thought. Hilarious.

I turn to my aunt. She's staring at the gory mess that was her brother.

"You saved us," I whisper. "All of us."

"Not him," she whispers back.

"He couldn't be saved."

"I know." A sigh shudders out from her very core. "I knew after he killed Mike that I'd have to kill him. I should've done it sooner, but…" She shakes her head. "It doesn't matter. His mother's family will always hate us and seek revenge. Mike and George's rivalry will never end, not even in death."

Her words sink into the pit of my stomach. She's right and there's nothing I can do about it.

My phone buzzes. I pull it from my pocket and see Tony's name on the screen. My throat tightens as my eyes squeeze shut. He's alive and so am I. We survived our father's sins and our uncle's vendetta. I answer with, "Yeah, hi, we're okay."

"What happened? We had the parking garage staked out, and all the guards suddenly collapsed. Was that you?"

"It was us." I decide not to specify who "us" is because that's a conversation.

"We're in the building now, on our way up." He pauses. "The Traitor?"

"Dead."

"How?"

"Us. Too much to say on the phone. I'll explain later."

As I hang up, Penny gestures for me to join her. She nods toward the unconscious crowd. "We released George's hold on them, but they could still on his side, right?"

I think of his mother's family who bankrolled this operation, and of his wife, my cousin, pregnant with his twin sons. Convenient pawns for the next battle. "Maybe not all of them, but some of them, definitely."

"We should disarm them."

I look at Aaron with his bent head and tense shoulders. *I need to talk to him first.*

Go ahead. Kai and Cat can help me.

I go to Aaron. Kai leaves his side and joins Penny and Auntie Cat, gathering weapons from Uncle George's unconscious goons.

"Hey," I say.

"Hey." He doesn't blink.

"Tony's on his way up. Jeremiah, too, probably."

He receives the news with a blank face. Then he juts his

chin at the sea of fallen pawns. "What about those assholes? Are they dead?"

"No. They should be fine. Just not under his control anymore."

He scoffs. "They liked being under his control."

How does he know that? I almost ask, 'Did you?' but that's way too loaded of a question. "Um, I'm sorry we had to kill your dad."

"Don't be. I'm not."

"Did you know he was going to kill you?"

Instead of answering, he gestures for me to follow him behind the dais.

He leads me to a long, dark corridor with closed doors. When we reach the end, he tries opening the last door, but it's locked. I motion him to step aside. It takes little effort to power up the Yang Pearl and aim the Dragon Shout at the handle. It blasts open. Frozen cold air escapes, as well as something else. The sweet-sour stench of death. I push open the door. The fluorescent lights flicker on, revealing an empty room, without furniture, carpeting, or windows. As the door swings fully open, I see five bodies, three men and two women piled against a wall as if tossed by careless hands. One of them is Leung Hoi-Yan. My stomach drops as acid burns my throat.

"What the hell?" I press my fingers to my nose as I speak. "Who are they?"

"His followers. People loyal to him." Aaron lips press tight before he continues. "He drained them of their *chi*. That's why he was so powerful. He was a fucking vampire. Anyway, he told me he was gonna do the same to me and Kai, and you and Penny, and everyone. He bragged that your *chi*, yours and Penny's, would make him even more powerful and that no one could defeat him."

I close the door, but Aaron doesn't move, despite the stench still leaking out. His face is tight with the effort to hold back emotion. "Why did he do that? Why did he show me? I mean, I'm his son. Was it to punish me? Would he really have done that?"

I want to lie, but I've been lied to so much in my life, I can't stand doing the same to him. "Yeah. I'm sorry. I don't think we were his family anymore. We became enemies and obstacles. He wanted us gone so he could start his new life." He looks down as I speak and doesn't reply when I finish. I can't think of anything to make him feel better except, "But he failed, and we lived, so fuck him."

Aaron snorts. "Gold Dragon. How fucked up was that?"

Footsteps and voices sound from the outer penthouse. Are Uncle George's people waking up? We hurry down the hall and have guns pointed at us as we enter the open space. I'm not afraid, though, because they belong to the Beggar Clan.

"Stand down," Jeremiah hollers across the room at the two camouflage-clad men holding us at bay.

They lower their weapons and we lower our hands. Other Beggars stand guard around the perimeter of the room while members of the Two Dragon Clan contain Uncle George's people, who are finally coming to their senses. Uncle Roy is hugging Auntie Cat. Penny and Kai ignore them all as they stare out a window. From their intense expressions and the tilt of their heads, it's obvious they're not talking about the amazing view.

Tony looms over his former father, staring down without blinking. I walk toward him, but Jeremiah comes striding over to block my way. I roll my eyes because does he have to do this, right now, in the middle of all the death and destruction? Yeah, he does, because he's not his father. I nod for Aaron to join our brother before facing my frenemy.

Jeremiah plants his staff on the floor with a militant thud. "Good to see you alive, kid."

"Your lucky day."

"So, you did all this, huh?"

I shrug, because I know saying nothing will bug the shit out of him.

He attempts an alpha male eye lock. I bat my eyelashes because I'm so done. Then he leans closer, speaking in that burnt gravel tone. "I don't care what kind of magic powers you got, kid. Our agreement stands. You try taking over, you'll face the entire Beggar Clan."

"It's all yours. The whole toy box. Have fun." I try stepping around him and he blocks my way again.

So over it. I raise my hand and, with almost no effort, use the Yang Pearl to shove him aside. He stumbles, pivoting on his staff as he attempts to maintain his balance. I stroll past him with a smirk and feel his eyes burn a hole in my back. It'll never be over for him, but that's too bad.

Then I stop because Tony and Aaron are talking and I don't want to interrupt them. They both look so much like my dad. Maybe that's the real reason Uncle George wanted to kill his own son. He couldn't bear the resemblance to his hated twin.

Aaron's shoulders start shaking. He bites his lip to keep from crying. Tony embraces him. His eyes close and a single tear slips down his cheek.

I take a deep breath to contain my emotions. Whatever happens next, this at least makes it all worthwhile.

Penny

The view really is grand. You can see almost the entire Bay Area. That being said, I'd hate to live in a place like this, trapped in a sterile, glass cage. Kai stares at that view as I tell him the truth about our mother and the curse. Telling him now feels wrong, but telling him later, once he relaxes and believes all is well, would be worse.

He's silent while I speak, pressing his hands into the glass as if wanting to leave his mark and let the world know he was there and survived.

When I finish, he keeps his gaze fixed on the Bay Bridge. "I felt it when Mum's curse entered him. I don't know how, cuz I was under his control, but I knew what it was." He turns to face me, his hazel eyes hard as marble. "We wouldn't have been up on the roof if you guys hadn't lied to us."

"I'm sorry. I didn't want to lie to you. Neither did Ba. Mum…" I shake my head, trying to find the right words. "She was so afraid. You know how she gets. She thought if you didn't know, she wouldn't have to worry about you."

"Look how that turned out." He presses his full weight

against the window before pushing off, leaving smudged handprints behind.

"Please don't be mad at her. Everything that's happened is punishment enough. She can barely speak. She'll never sing again."

The chill in his eyes thaws. He knows as well as I do that despite being an amazing musician Bridie's first passion is singing. Being robbed of that truly was losing a piece of her soul. "It's probably better I didn't know. After they captured us, dead wanker over there started grilling me for everything I knew. And I told him. He would've known about the curse and maybe been able to stop you."

"But you wouldn't have been up on the roof."

He shrugs. "Aaron and I would've been up on the roof the moment Tony gave us permission. I don't think there was a way to prevent this from happening."

I allow myself a brief smile. Quick to anger and quick to forgiveness. He got that from Gerry. Bridie, Matthew, and I are the grudge holders.

Speaking of grudges, Jeremiah bears down on us, his pounding staff leaving scuffs on the hardwood floor. It takes all my willpower not to roll my eyes. Is he expecting gratitude? He'll never have that from me, not after selling me out to my uncle. Still, I think of his father, less than two months dead, and how that must feel for him. Jeremiah puts on a blustery show, but he must still be mourning. I need to muster a gracious word. The best I can come up with is "Fancy meeting you here."

"How'd you do this?" he demands.

I squint as if confused. "I didn't do anything."

He scowls. "Don't be cute, Penny. I know you and Lennon share some kind of power. What is it?"

Did Mad Maud throw me over the bridge? No. She

wouldn't do that. But that doesn't mean there weren't others in the London Abode who saw or heard and peached.

"Do you believe in dragons?" I ask.

His scowl deepens.

"Well, you should." I attempt to walk past him, but he blocks the way.

"I order you to tell me."

"I just did."

"Your uncle owes me. So does the Two Dragon Clan. You'll pay off that debt by telling me."

"Any debt my family or the Two Dragon Clan owes you has been paid in full. You're the undisputed Head of the Crossroads until someone other than Lennon takes it from you."

I stroll around him. Kai, who'd been watching our exchange like a tennis match, trots over to my side and whispers, "Like a boss."

I smile because who doesn't enjoy being rewarded with their little brother's admiration? It quickly fades as we approach Lennon's family. We won, but nobody looks happy or triumphant. I mean, I'm happy, but I'm not related to George Lau. I wouldn't feel any joy if it was Uncle Christy lying dead at my feet, despite all he's done to me and my family. Tony is on the phone, speaking in Cantonese, his brow creased. Kai trots off to join Aaron. Lennon comes to my side, but we don't speak aloud since the Beggars are nearby.

Tony's talking to Second Elder. What happened here, happened everywhere. Whoever was under Uncle George's control all collapsed at the same time.

It's crazy to think we're that powerful.

We're not.

That's true. Even with the pearls, it took the additional boost of dragon energy to defeat George. *I wonder where those damn dragons are.*

You don't sense them?

I haven't tried… I reach out and find them almost immediately. Jade Dragon and Master Stoorworm, both the size of Peregrine falcons, are directly below us, perched on the floor of the dragon gate. *So, they were here the whole time?*

I guess so.

Are they happy with the outcome?

Dunno.

Are you happy? I ask them.

They reply by flying away, heading west, toward the ocean. I roll my eyes. Not that I was expecting much of an answer.

Dragons don't do happy, says Lennon.

Also true. Maybe satisfied would've been a better word, but I'm not in the mood to pursue them.

The sad task of cleanup begins. Jeremiah offers to dispose of the bodies and Tony politely declines. I don't blame him. Jeremiah won't piss on you if you're on fire unless you pay him. Since there's no further advantage to sticking around, the Beggar Clan departs. Lennon watches them leave with bitter eyes. I know what he's thinking. This would've been so different with John Walks Long. It can still be different. I hope with all my soul that Helena challenges Jeremiah and wins.

As George's henchmen come to their senses, they're escorted to view his uncovered body. Tony notes their reactions, those relieved and those dismayed. He releases the former. The latter, escorted to another part of the penthouse where Roy is waiting to grill them.

"What are you going to do with them?" I ask Lennon. We're perched on the top step of the dais, beneath the dragon throne, leaning against a matching pair of stone lions. He's watching Tony do his grim business because he has to as Dragon Son. I'm there as support even though I'd rather be with Kai and Aaron, sitting cross-legged next to the windows, away from gory George.

Lennon shrugs. "Banish them from the clan and let them

go. The only alternative is killing them and I'm not up for that."

There's a bigger question I need to ask: what are we going to do with the pearls? George's amulet feels like it's burning a hole in my pocket, but the idea of giving it to someone else, even Lennon… I can't. I need to look at it, like, right now.

"Where's the bathroom?" I ask.

"Good question." Lennon sits up, his eyes tracking the guy Tony just dismissed. "Hey, you." The guy flinches. "Yeah, you. Where's the bathroom?"

The guy blinks at this inane demand before replying in Cantonese.

Lennon turns to me. "Behind this stage, there's a hallway. The bathroom is the third door on the left. Don't go into the last room. Trust me."

I trust him. I have no more stomach for his uncle's evil deeds.

Inside the bathroom, I lock the door and lean on it for good measure. Then I unzip my coat pocket and remove the amulet. I brush my fingertips over the surface of the Wisdom and Summoning Pearls, feeling the thrum of green-red energy. Similar, yet different from the opalescent blue that shimmers from Jade Dragon. How did the Two Dragon Clan wind up with Master Stoorworm's pearls? Was it an accident? No. Dragons don't do accidents. They planted their scheme among our clans and waited and watched for centuries. Why?

My thumb presses a little too hard and the Wisdom Pearl comes loose. No, not loose. I tug a little harder and pull it free of the amulet. That's when I realize the surface of the amulet is magnetized, holding the pearls in place. Behind each setting is a small hole, securing each pearl's chain within the amulet. George must've had this custom made so he could use the pearls separately and together.

There's a clasp on the side of the amulet, allowing easier

access to the chains. I open it and thread the Wisdom Pearl's chain back in. I can't give it back to Lennon or the Two Dragon Clan. It's not theirs, but it's not mine, either. All I know is that I need to hold on to it for now.

I tug on the Summoning Pearl, releasing it from the amulet. It isn't mine, either. I have to give it to someone.

Must give it.

I leave the bathroom and return to the main room. After glancing around, I spot Cat in a far corner, staring out the window. Her family murdered each other over these pearls. Does she blame the dragons who gave them such dangerous weapons? Or does she blame the ones who couldn't control their lust for power? I try to veer away, but I can't. My feet move regardless of my will. She turns to me as I join her, expectation on her face. She holds out her palm to receive the Summoning Pearl.

As she places it around her neck, she asks, "When?"

"I don't know," I reply. I don't even know what 'when' is. Only that there is a when and that I'll be there, and so will she.

We exchange nods, and I walk across the room, climbing the stairs to sit beside Lennon.

"Do you know when?" I ask.

He shakes his head, no question in his eyes.

Yeah, this is so weird. It's not even a compulsion, it's a thing, something that's a fact that hasn't happened yet. A phrase from Shakespeare comes to mind.

Ill met by moonlight, proud Titania.

I take out my phone and open the browser to check the phases of the moon. It will be full on Wednesday, tomorrow. I show Lennon and he nods.

Tomorrow.

Lennon

"Where are the pearls?"

That's the first thing Tony says to me when we get back to the *kongsi*. Not, 'Are you ok?' 'Are you tired, hungry?' 'I love you.' Lol. Yeah, right. It's all good. I know he loves me. I love him, too. It's what keeps me from telling him to piss off. I mean, yeah, he had the decency to wait until I used the bathroom, but then he barged into my room without knocking. He's gotta stop doing that.

I pull a T-shirt over my head before replying. "We have them."

"You and Penny."

"Yeah." Technically, that's true. She and I have three of the pearls. I don't tell him that Penny gave the Summoning Pearl to Auntie Cat. He doesn't need to know that. Not yet.

"The pearls need to be secured. There's a safe in our father's office. Only I know the combination. I'll give it to you as well. We'll put the other three pearls there."

"No."

Tony doesn't blink. Neither do I.

"You can change the combination, so that only you know it," he says.

"No."

Still no blinking. I don't pull rank because I don't have to. Tony knows. He's the one who made me be the Dragon Son. He won't show regret, even if it's hitting him like a freight train right now.

He takes a breath. "What are you going to do with the pearls?"

"Me?" I shrug. "Nothing. That's up to Jade Dragon."

"He's spoken to you about them?"

"Yes." Okay, that is a lie. He hasn't spoken to me in words. It's more like gut-feeling, but Tony isn't good with feelings.

"What did he say?"

"He said he'll tell us what he wants done with the pearls tomorrow."

"Tomorrow?"

"Yup."

That doesn't sit well with him. He wants to believe our ancestor is decisive and precise. He still doesn't get that Jade Dragon is wild, values logic over righteousness, and is also kind of a dick.

There's a tap on the door.

"Come in," I say before Tony can speak.

May pokes her head in. "Dinner is ready."

"Thanks," I say. "I'll be there in a minute."

Tony shoots me a narrow glare before following his wife. I sit on my bed and sigh. I wish Penny was still here. She and her family left almost as soon as we returned to the *kongsi*. It was painful watching Bridie, overjoyed with the safe return of her children, while still fragile and heartbroken over the loss of her voice. When she said she wanted to go home, no one could say no. Not even the motherfucking Dragon Son.

My phone buzzes. I grab it and check the screen. The sight of Penny's message warms the chill in my heart.

> Want to go to the studio tomorrow?

> Oh hell yeah. What time?

> Noon?

As soon as I hit send on my thumbs up, I relax. I don't feel the need to talk more. What we have to say to each other needs to be done in person.

After dinner, over Tony's objections, I return home with Auntie Cat and Uncle Roy. It isn't really my home though, any more than the *kongsi*. It's just a place where some of my stuff is, especially my scooter.

The next day, Auntie Cat nods serenely as I head out the door. Uncle Roy makes no objections. He must know she has the Summoning Pearl. Maybe they want some alone time before whatever happens, happens. I know the feeling.

Penny is waiting for me on the steps of her apartment building. She's wearing Doc Martens with striped socks up to her knees, black bike shorts, and her crazy, colorful sweater with a scarf wrapped around her neck. As I pull up to the curb, she stands, smiles, and skips down the stairs. I take off my helmet to greet her and she kisses me on the mouth.

Wow. That gives me feelings. Like I don't want to stop. Ever. I want to wrap my arms around her, but she takes a step back. That's when I notice that behind her smile, there's a sadness in her eyes and a droop to her shoulders.

"You okay?" I ask.

She nods.

"Your mom?"

She shakes her head. "I used the Yin Pearl on her this morning. She can talk better now, but she can't sing. She never will." Her voice cracks. Tears fill her eyes.

"I'm sorry," I whisper.

"It is what it is. She needs time to heal."

We all do, but those dragons won't give it to us. All we have is today.

After putting on her helmet, Penny slides behind me and I pull out to the street. I give a silent sigh as her arms wind around me, tension easing from my body. I forgot how good this feels, me, her, my scooter, and the entire city before us. This sense of freedom… I need it like I need water. I can't live without it.

When we reach the Kinetic Collective, it finally feels like I've come home. The handful of artists lounging in the common area barely glance at us as we walk in. At the far end of the warehouse, Mona commands the forge as Junkyard Metallurgy builds their latest commission, a giant, fiberoptic Christmas tree.

"Too bad you didn't get to see Doris the Spider in action," I say as we climb the stairs.

"I did. They posted the video on their website," Penny replies. "It looked brilliant. Maybe we can volunteer if they resurrect her next Halloween."

"Actually, Mona says they're taking her to Burning Man next year."

"Even better."

Just the thought of me and Penny going to Burning Man makes my heart beat faster. That has to happen.

My grin fades as I open the door to the studio and have to push aside the spray paint cans that had rolled against it. I forgot about the damn earthquake. The shelves holding my art supplies are bare, their contents scattered across the studio. The rack holding Penny's spray-painted clothing has tipped over, with T-shirts and leggings splayed all over the floor. It's a buzzkill. We both sigh and get to work.

It takes about an hour to straighten everything up. We're starving, so we head to our favorite sandwich shop, Banh Jovi, to get lemongrass tofu sandwiches and iced *cafe sua da*. Then we head for the end of the pier and sit with our legs dangling over the side while we eat.

A cold breeze whips around us, so we nestle against each other for warmth. I have that feeling again of wanting to hold on to this moment forever, the spicy lemongrass mingled with the sweet, creamy coffee, the blue sky puffy with white clouds, the waves below us lapping against the pier, the dull roar of traffic on the Bay Bridge overhead, and the soft-strong feeling of Penny's body against mine. What could be more perfect?

After finishing her sandwich, Penny reaches into her pocket and pulls out the Wisdom Pearl. It dangles before her like a globe of red-green fire. "I wonder why Master Stoorworm gave this to the Two Dragon Clan instead of the Strowlers."

"You're sure it's from him?"

She takes my hand, drops the pearl and its chain into my palm and closes my fingers around it.

I close my eyes and allow my *chi* to flow into that energy. It's dark green with ruby red eyes, and the scent of sulfur, and the flap of wings… Wings. Jade Dragon doesn't have wings.

"He's here," I announce. Undulating beneath the bay, a creature of the deep, despite those wings. He and my ancestor have that in common.

Penny opens my hand and retrieves the pearl. She whispers, "Can you hear what he's saying?" She pauses. "Not hear. Feel. Can you feel it?"

I nod. "Tony's going to be pissed."

"It doesn't belong to Tony. Or you. Or me."

"Who does it belong to?"

"Him. I guess."

For some reason, that answer doesn't seem right, but it doesn't matter. I know what she has to do.

Penny takes a deep breath and flings the Wisdom Pearl into the bay.

It hits the water but doesn't sink. Sunlight glistens off the gold chain as it floats on the surface. We exchange worried glances. What if it washes back to shore and someone finds it? Then the waves around it churn. A whirlpool forms, sucking the Wisdom Pearl into its depths.

A whirlpool. Circles upon circles.

I no longer see the water. I see a whirlpool made of stone. No, a coil. No. What's the right word? The circles aren't concentric. They form a winding path, like a maze…

Or a labyrinth, says Penny.

Okay, so, whatever this is, a vision, I guess, she sees it, too.

The vision expands. We're standing in a clearing at the edge of a cliff. It's night and I can make out the lights of the Golden Gate Bridge in the distance. Ocean waves crash below, coating us with mist. The sharp breeze chills my dampened skin.

Stones litter the ground as if scattered by a giant hand. Without thinking, I join Penny, picking up the rocks and setting them in an ever-expanding pattern. I feel the weight of each stone, and if it's dry and caked with dirt or wet and slimy with moss. We're silent beyond the sound of our feet crunching the gravelly ground as we search out rocks and set them in place until they form that same labyrinth. The full moon hangs overhead, glowing like a spotlight on our handiwork. I know the time, not as time, but as a feeling. When I must be there. When we must be there.

I blink. It's daylight and I'm sitting on the edge of the dock, staring at the Oakland hills across the bay. Penny gasps beside me. She raises her hands and I stare at mine as well, covered with damp, gritty soil. We examine our shoes, at the mud embedded in the crevices of the soles.

"We were there," I whisper.

"That wasn't the dragons," she whispers back. "That was fairy magic."

I nod because I know she's right. I don't know how I know, but I do. "It's like we traveled in time, but we didn't. Like we were there before we were there."

What I'm saying doesn't make sense, but Penny replies as if it does. "That's how the fairies work, but why? Is Leannán Sidhe involved with Master Stoorworm again?" She shakes her head. "Lands End. That's here in the city, yeah?"

I nod.

"Have you been there?"

I shudder, shaking off the effects of the vision. "Yeah. Once. Auntie Cat took me to the Legion of Honor Museum for the Matisse exhibit. They - my parents - didn't like me doing art stuff, so we told them she was taking me on a hike to Lands End, and that's what we did after we saw the exhibit. The trail is next to the museum."

My phone buzzes. I pull it out of my pocket and read the message from Auntie Cat.

Did you see the labyrinth?

I show Penny.

She nods without surprise. "When we go to Lands End, we bring our families. That's what I felt... what I know. It must have something to do with us and the pearls."

What did Jade Dragon say?

What I give remains until the day has come.

Maybe today is that day. Cool. I won't have to explain to Tony why we chucked the Wisdom Pearl into the bay. And if Jade Dragon takes back his pearls, then I won't have to be the Dragon Son anymore. Even more cool.

Except why would he want the pearls back now? Is that a good or a bad thing? And why are fairies involved?

I text with Auntie Cat, but she has nothing to add except she and Roy will meet us at Lands End tonight. Then I put away my phone and sigh. What I really want to do is go back to the studio and lie on my cot with Penny in my arms, but those damn dragons won't cut us any slack.

Penny gazes out over the bay as she speaks. "I love you. Whatever happens tonight, I don't want to lose you again."

I still feel that loss. That time we said goodbye, thinking we'd never see each other again. "You won't. I love you, too. So much. I wish I had the words to say how much."

She chews her lip for a moment before turning toward me, her green eyes shining emeralds. "If you must steal, then steal my heart and make it yours. If you must lie, then lie in my arms every night. And if you must cheat, then cheat death and be mine forevermore."

That's it. Those exact words. "What is that? What you just said."

"It's what Strowler lovers say to bind themselves to each other."

"Should I say it, too?"

"Only if you want to bind yourself to me."

"Is it like magic?"

"Of course."

Her smile is a hook on my heart. I think of the first time I saw her dance and how I thought she looked like a fairy. Magical. I think that's when I fell in love with her. I reach for her hands and, with her help, repeat those words that bind us, heart and soul.

Nothing will tear us apart again, not even those damn dragons.

Penny

Love. That's all I feel when Lennon drops me off in front of my apartment building. Our parting kiss is a soft touch of the lips and a shared smile. Whatever happens tonight, we've been through too much to lose this love now.

Inside, music drifts down the stairwell. I recognize the tune, Wanderlust, one of Gerry's instrumental compositions, with an Irish-Arabic fusion sound. Inside the apartment, Matthew and Kai strum their guitars while Bridie plays the fiddle, her eyes closed as if lost in another world. I find my bag of penny whistles, pull out the high D, and join them.

For so long, it had been me, Mum, and Kai playing through our memories. I almost forgot the rich, full sound, like colors vibrating in the air, that Matthew brings to our music. Gerry took those colors and gave them an edge. He didn't play to make people comfortable. He played to make people feel alive.

Bridie brought the passion, then and now. Tears roll down her cheeks until she finishes the song with the last note. Her fiddle collapses into her lap as she bows her head and weeps.

She's cried a lot, but she's lost so much, and gained so much as well. Tears glitter in Matthew's eyes as he stands to go to her. I shake my head to stop him before sliding across the couch and placing my hand on her shoulder. I close my eyes, concentrating on the healing power of the Yin Pearl, strength and love flowing through me and into her.

She lifts her head and gives a resolute snuffle before rasping, "Tonight?"

"Tonight," I confirm. I glance at Kai and Matthew, and they nod. They know. I don't ask how. These pearls have touched us all. Whatever lingers within is telling us tonight.

"I'll let you know when it's time," I continue. "We're going to Lands End, so dress for a hike."

"To the labyrinth?" Kai asks as he sets down his guitar.

I drop my pennywhistle. I don't want to alarm my skittish mother, so I keep my tone casual as I bend over to pick it up. "Labyrinth?"

"I had a dream last night that I was walking a labyrinth next to the ocean, under the moonlight…" His voice trails off with his shrug. "I don't remember the rest." His eyes widen. "Hey, you think the dragons were trying to send me a message or something?"

The pinprick in my chest sparks as he speaks. Kai dreamed of the labyrinth last night before Lennon and I had our vision this afternoon. Why? And why only him?

"I'll bet I'm the only person in the world descended from both those scaly dudes. I mean, until you and Lennon have kittens."

"Shut up," I snap, trying to deflect the worry creeping into me. Does that make Kai special to them? Or do they even care? It's so hard to know with them.

"Do those dragons want something from him?" asks Bridie, her tight voice straining with fear.

I squeeze her shoulder, channeling a little more courage into her as I speak. "They want something from all of us. There's no avoiding it. If they wanted to hurt us, they would've done it before now." Should I tell them about the labyrinth Lennon and I built in our vision? If I do, Bridie will dig in her heels and refuse to allow any of us to go to Lands End tonight. Thing is, if we don't go voluntarily, the dragons will take us forcefully and I'm not up for that. "Let's not face it on empty bellies. How about I start dinner?"

Her shoulders straighten, and a smile brightens her face, though her voice remains just above a whisper. "No. Matty and I are making bangers and mash, just like the old days."

My mouth waters. Matthew always made the best onion gravy and got the sausage skins the perfect amount of crisp.

When we finally sit at the kitchen table, my first mouthful is blissful proof he hasn't lost his touch. Last night, when we got home, we ordered pizza since no one was in any shape to cook. Now, sitting around the table with a proper meal, everything feels so right... minus one. Our family will never be entirely right without Gerry. I wish his ghostly presence had followed us here so I could sense his happiness at seeing us all together again. But no, he either remained behind with Gareth or continued his journey to the everlasting.

I shiver, thinking of how his brother, Oren, spread his ashes at the crossroads. As if that, or anything, would stop Gerry from going where he pleases.

"Thinking of your Da?" whispers Bridie.

I nod. She squeezes my hand. Matthew takes my other hand. Kai reaches out to his parents until we're joined in a sort of prayer for what was and what will be.

After dinner and dishes, the other three return to their music. I go to my room, open the window, and climb out to the fire escape/balcony. I settle in the folding chair and watch fog enshroud the city. Will we even be able to see the full moon? I draw my knees to my chest, though I'm not cold. Dragon fire spreads through my body. I close my eyes and picture Lands End, where the ocean meets the bay, mingles, and becomes one. I walk the labyrinth's maze-like spirals, the damp ground uneven beneath my feet. Here the ocean meets the land, its waves battering, eroding, wanting, demanding, to press on. Ocean, bay, and land meet here, separate, but also one. I sense a presence in the center of the labyrinth, watching me, her laughter like a shiver of silver bells…

It's time.

My eyes pop open. The fog is gone, and the moon shines brightly overhead. I get up and stretch, my limbs stiff from sitting entranced. A week ago, this would've been terrifying. Now, it feels normal. Will it still feel that way after I give up the Yin Pearl? I place my palm over its cool surface and feel my heartbeat match its thrum. How can I give it up? I can't. It's not mine to release into the hands of another.

I'm not surprised to find my family in the front parlor, coats on, waiting for me. I lace up my Doc Martens, grab a jacket, and we're out the door to whatever awaits us.

Bridie drives and I navigate by phone as we head for the north-western edge of the city, past the Golden Gate Bridge, to the battered cliffs above the ocean's shore. We park on a dead-end road next to the Legion of Honor Museum–its palace-like walls glowing marble white under the moonlight. There are no other cars nearby, meaning Lennon and his family haven't yet arrived. We follow signs pointing to the Lands End Trail. The cement walkway becomes a dirt path, narrowing as it leads us into a wooded area.

Kai leads the way, his feet unfaltering at the forks in the trail, as if he's been here before. The roar of the ocean greets us as we leave the woods and pick our way down a steep, uneven incline toward the water. The moon hangs overhead like a lamp lighting our way. In the distance, the Golden Gate Bridge casts an orange glow, reflecting off the water. We reach a clearing where we find the stone labyrinth and something else. A figure, a person, perched at the edge of the cliff.

My breath stops first. Then my feet. No, it can't be... How is he here? Do the others see him?

Bridie, Matthew, and Kai stare at the figure with tilted heads and narrowed eyes. They recognize him, not trusting what they see.

The figure rises, graceful as a cat, and turns toward us. The cold wind whips at his unruly curls, obscuring his face. He rakes a hand across his brow, revealing those blue eyes shaded by thick black eyebrows, that long nose, and those full lips pulled back in a grin that's both devilish and apologetic.

I launch myself across the clearing, reaching out to grasp his arms. He's solid. Real.

My father.

Gerry.

Alive.

He embraces me, kissing my head, and rocking me back and forth while whispering, "My darling girl. My Penny Lane."

He feels like him, slender, but all muscle, and only a couple of inches taller than me now. He smells of the ocean and is wearing the same clothes from my dreams, those same clothes he'd died in. Then I sense it, the glow in his chest, a sharp seed of dragon fire, and over that, he wears around his neck the Wisdom Pearl.

I don't realize I'm crying until I pull away and ask in a wavering voice, "How?"

He shrugs. "Those dragons weren't done with me."

There's so much in those words, but before I can ask, we're surrounded by our family. Hugs, laughter, tears, anger swirl around us in a wild energy. Kai bounces with happiness as Bridie collapses into Gerry's arms while Matthew grips his shoulder and says, "Bastard," over and over.

As everyone calms down, I ask, "What happened? How is

this possible? Oren told us he spread your ashes at the crossroads."

"That's one thing I'm grateful for. Oren spent his life waiting for that moment, his ultimate control over me, deciding my eternity, and those dragons robbed him of it." Gerry gives a short, bitter bark of a laugh before settling on a craggy boulder. I join him, leaning against him so I can assure myself he's still real. Bridie, Matthew, and Kai sit on the ground, huddled together against the wind, their incredulous eyes fixed on Gerry's face as he tells his tale.

"When we fell out that window and hit the ground, I died. My body, I mean. Something snatched me, my soul, whatever you want to call it, away, enclosing it in this place..." He stops and shakes his head. "I don't know what to call it. Just... energy. I was aware, for want of a better word. I could see what was happening outside of me... my body. They dragged us inside the London *kongsi* and did a strip search. Every orifice. Mad feckers. The Dragon Son scanned our bodies with the Yang Pearl, searching for the other pearls, but that same energy hid the Yin Pearl inside Matthew. They went spare, throttling our bodies before turning the *kongsi* upside down and sideways. They took to the gutters and even the sewers before coming up empty. Eventually, they tossed my body into a car and dumped me outside the Strowler encampment. Later, Oren showed up to claim me. He got as far as a crematorium, and when he went inside to make arrangements, I, my body, disappeared."

"Why did he tell us he had you cremated?" I ask.

He gets that look of lingering fear associated with his oldest brother. "Cruelty. Why else? He believed I was alive, had been playing dead, and that I'd scarpered. Not just from him, but from everyone. That I was coward enough to abandon my family to save my skin. He wanted me gone and didn't want anyone looking for me, so he kept it to himself."

"After a while, I realized Master Stoorworm was keeping me alive in a hidden cave beneath the sea. The task took so much of his energy, he could do little else. Slowly, I healed, but the only thing that could reunite body and soul was this." He tugs on the gold chain around his neck and pulls out the Wisdom Pearl.

I gasp. "Why? Why didn't he just take it from George and give it to you?"

Gerry's mouth pulls sideways. "Why do those dragons do anything?"

"To make us strive and suffer so we'll gain wisdom from experience."

"Or some such shite, yeah. Except I think they tired of waiting. Master Stoorworm let me loose to drop wee hints, though he kept me from saying all I could."

"What can you say now? What do they want?"

"Us."

As he says that word, voices echo above us, along with the crunch of feet on rocky ground. Aaron leads the way out of the woods and down the incline, followed by Lennon, Tony, Cat, and Roy. They halt when they reach us, their faces perplexed at the sight of Gerry, all but Lennon's.

He sucks in a gasp before breathing out, "How?"

My father grins. "How else?"

Lennon's eyes fill with tears. His voice breaks as he says, "But my dad, he killed you."

"That he did, but you brought me back. You, my girl, all of you, knowing or not."

Tony's eyes narrow. "You're Penny's father?"

"Gerry Kestrel, at your service," Da says with a tip of his head.

"I'm Tony Lau. Lennon's older brother."

"I know who you are."

"How? We've never met."

"In dreams. Yours and mine."

Tony's face goes blank, as if he almost remembers. Then he gives his head a little shake, refusing to believe in such nonsense. "You're wearing the Wisdom Pearl. Did Penny give it to you?"

"You know better than that, lad."

"Jade Dragon gave it to you?"

Gerry shakes his head. "It's not his to give."

Cat steps forward. "The other dragon, Master Stoorworm, he wanted you to have it. Just like he wanted me to have this." She pulls the Summoning Pearl out from under her jacket. "These pearls belong to Master Stoorworm, not Jade Dragon. He gave them to the Two Dragon Clan so we would eventually find each other."

Skepticism fills Tony's eyes. "Why would an Irish dragon want anything to do with our family?"

"Dragons don't have nationalities," says Lennon.

His brother glares at him. "Jade Dragon is our family dragon."

"You still don't get it. He's not our dragon. We're his humans."

Behind us, Kai walks the labyrinth. I huff with annoyance. Why does he have to be a little prat and muck about when things are so serious? As I watch him, though, I realize his movement isn't random. He takes deliberate steps through each twist of the maze as if entranced.

I go to the opening of the labyrinth, but as I try stepping onto the path, I'm stopped. Not by any force. I simply can't go inside.

"Kai?" I call out.

He doesn't reply. Doesn't even glance at me. When he reaches the center, he stops and cocks his head as if listening to someone. Then he does look at me, calmly, even sweetly, and announces, "They're here."

Master Stoorworm swoops across the strait, his golden underbelly skimming the surface before he rises above Lands End, his dark green leathery wings sending gusts of cold air as he flaps to stay aloft. Below him, waves stir and swirl until a giant whirlpool forms.

Water rains down on us as Jade Dragon rises from the depths. Though wingless like a sea serpent, he's able to hover in the sky, his teal-blue body undulating with the effort.

Everyone gasps and recoils as they appear. Everyone but Kai, who stares with solemn eyes at his forefathers. I grasp my arms and shiver, though not from the water that soaked me or the wind that chills me. Kai, their sole descendent. This is about him.

Gerry's hands go to his hips as he shouts, "Are you feckers going to tell us what you're playing at?"

Those feckers don't reply. We puny humans exchange uneasy glances.

Lennon comes to my side and whispers, "Jade Dragon's ignoring me. Can you talk to Master Stoorworm?"

I don't answer because I can't. I'm frozen in place, facing

my brother, who remains at the center of the stones. Lennon turns abruptly and walks along the edge of the circle. Gerry and Cat move in a similar propelled motion until we're all standing equidistant from each other around the labyrinth. Our placement can't be random, with me facing my father and Lennon facing his aunt.

A circle of power emits around the ring, connecting us to each other, together, complete at last.

The dragons fly over us, shrinking down to a size allowing them to settle on the hill above. Silence, except for the roar of the ocean, the lap of waves, and the stirring of the wind. Our families must be frozen in place, too.

Seconds pass, like the ticking of a clock. We're waiting for the time, and when that time comes…

The pinprick in my chest becomes a hot coal, so painful I'd scream if I could. Its heat spreads through my body before flowing into the Yin Pearl. Around the circle, our pearls glow, softly at first, before gaining intensity. I can see Kai's face clearly now, so pale, as if drained of blood, and his eyes so wide. I catch his gaze and hold it, unable to help him, but at least reassure him I'm here, with him, for whatever happens.

Sis, I'm scared. I hear this as clearly as if he's beside me.

I know. I am, too.

What are they doing to us? To me?

I don't know. I…

The glow of the pearls becomes beams of light, conduits of energy pouring into Kai. I want to scream and struggle, but all I can do is watch it happen. My brother's eyes close and an aura appears around him, glowing cyan, emerald, and magenta. It intensifies as the glow of the pearls diminishes, fades, and dissolves.

My throat tightens. The Yin Pearl. It's gone. My pinprick goes back to what it was, a tiny source of irritation and energy.

What power do I have now, if any? How can I save my brother?

A door appears behind Kai.

I blink, because I can, and search for a wall that isn't there. Just a plain, unpolished wood door, with a large gold ring at its center.

How? Why?

Kai turns and reaches for the ring.

No! I struggle to shout a warning, to make any sound at all, but can't.

He grasps the ring and knocks three times. Each knock sends a vibration through my soul.

The door opens and a woman steps out. The wind blows at her long, jet-black hair and simple, silken robe, revealing her bare arms, bare feet, and pointed ears. Her smile would seem almost tender if it weren't for the glimmer of mischief in her silver eyes.

I know who she is.

Blood of my blood.

Leannán Sidhe.

What does she want of my brother, my family, all of us?

The door disappears.

She lays her hand on Kai's shoulder, and the aura around him melts into a single amber glow. Then her hand slides off, and she journeys through the labyrinth. As she walks, she sings in a language unknown and her voice…

Ah, my heart aches at its beauty.

I don't understand the words of her song and yet the story unfolds as she sings.

"Two worlds exist, side-by-side, born together, not brethren.
One world, of humans, beasts, flora, fauna, life, death.

One world of fae, demigods, dragons, all things eldritch
and undying.
Nature made provision for each world.
One flawed and fertile, the other sublime and sterile.

"Magic flows through the eldritch world, allowing them
to shape it to their will.
Yet one thing cannot be summoned or compelled.
Life. Birth.
To attain fertility, they must enter the mortal world.
Where the flaws enchant them and the beings amuse
and anger them.

"Some lingered to live as gods, to toy with humans and
beasts.
To spread their seed recklessly.
Some offspring lived to return to the eldritch world.
Others died, abominable, or merely human, and
unmourned.
Then humans forged the perfect weapon.

"Iron
Does not burn or kill
As human lore would say.
Iron is its own magic, to weaken and deflect
That of eldritch beings.

"Disdain was our downfall.
Too late we learned and so we fled.
Back to our world, back to ourselves, our courts and
intrigues.
Only to discover
As the centuries passed, so did our ability to conceive.

"Immortal beings, still can we die
Through sword, poison, illness, and sorrow.
Our numbers dwindled, none more-so than the
dragons.
Always few, dispassionate, inquisitive, harsh
To the suffering and dying of their spawn.

"Until there were no more but two males.
Doomed to extinction
Until they hatched a plan to create a new brood.
They had not enough magic
Or enough of the natural world that can conceive.

"So, they mated, one with human, the other with fae.
Gifting pearls to those of sea dragon.
Second sight to those of sky dragon.
And they waited for the magic to quicken.
Through the generations, until they appeared.

"The Tinder - to wield the Summoning Pearl.
The Catalyst - to wield the Wisdom Pearl.
The Spark - to wield the Yin Pearl.
The Flame - to wield the Yang Pearl.
To pour their magic into the One.

"The Spawn!

"Born of sea dragon, sky dragon, fae, and human.
Of this One, many will come forth.
Eldritch beings, immune to iron, able to bear fruit.
Born at youth's end
Each according to their nature.

"Sea dragon, sky dragon, fae, and human.

"Each must grow, must walk the maze to attain their
eldritch flame.
Some will be torches who burn quickly, extinguished to
nothing.
Some will fear their flame, smother it, and die as
mortals.
Others will embrace their flame, growing in power
Until ready to make their way to the eldritch world.

"He of sea and he of sky
Shall remain in the mortal world.
Observing their spawn shed skin for scale
Destroying any who threatens the existence of all."

Leannán Sidhe reaches the end of the labyrinth. She
continues singing, though these words have no meaning, at
least not to me. She beckons, and Bridie and Matthew join her
as if tugged by an invisible rope. Leannán Sidhe lays her hands
on their shoulders. Their voices rise in song with hers. Tears
stream from Bridie's eyes, her tone strong and pure. What was
ripped from her soul by a curse now healed by her fairy
ancestor.

Leannán Sidhe's voice rises above theirs as she walks the
labyrinth once again.

"Mortal born, eldritch blood
Your time has come
Enter into your own."

Kai's aura bursts into what looks like a swarm of fireflies,
glowing with an amber fire. Most disperse, their trails dimin-
ishing as they spread across the sky in all directions. A few
propel directly at us.

I gasp, unable to run, struggle, or even swat the "firefly" as it burrows into my pinprick of power. Instead of heat, a cool shimmer of energy flows through me. I close my eyes and see a silver waterfall. I step into it, allowing it to drench me thoroughly, extinguishing what remains of the dragon fire.

I open my eyes and gasp again. Everything looks sharper, clearer, as if it's day rather than night. The leaves greener, the rocks sharp and smooth, each crag defined, and the wind and waves making their own music.

Leannán Sidhe's garments are threaded with silver, as is her hair, catching a multitude of colors. The scales of the dragons are more like prisms, shimmering off the luminosity of the immense pearls at their throats. Their slit, black pupils shaped like keyholes, surrounded by a burnt gold that radiates into a fiery red, mosaic-like pattern.

What other beauties of the world have I missed through my dull eyes? Everything! I need to see everything. This desire burns within me, cold, not hot.

Leannán Sidhe reaches the center of the labyrinth and releases Birdie and Matthew on either side of Kai. Their song ends. The wind blows and the waves roar, and everything is darker again.

The door reappears, opening of its own accord. Leannán Sidhe kisses Kai's cheek before stepping through. I try straining my neck to see what lies beyond, but it disappears before I can catch a glimpse.

The dragons rise and fly away, growing as they vanish into ocean and sky.

A collective gasp escapes us all. Bridie and Matthew embrace their son, who looks none the worse for wear. I turn to Lennon and the first thing I notice are his eyes.

He speaks first. "Penny. Your eyes are silver."

I reply, "So are yours."

What does it mean?

I look again at my family. Gerry has joined the others in

their embrace of their son. His eyes, as well as Bridie's and Matthew's, are silver. Kai's remains their usual hazel.

Tony, Aaron, and Roy join Cat. Their eyes are red, with black-gold slits for pupils. All but Aaron, whose eyes are still brown.

Lennon's mind brushes against mine. A cascade of relief overwhelms me. Whatever happened to us, we still share that. I don't think I could bear it if we didn't.

Do you see what I see? he asks.

Our eyes? Uh, yeah.

Not just that. It's who has what eyes.

Everyone on the Wayward Way has silver eyes and everyone on the Glory Road has red eyes. Everyone except Kai and Aaron. *Born at youth's end. Each according to their nature.*

Do you remember every word she said? he asks.

I nod.

Me, too. It's, like, engraved on my heart or something.

Blessings and curses are like that.

Is this a blessing or a curse?

Dunno. Could be both. I'm not sure what you call a spell cast centuries ago.

"Penny," Gerry calls out. His silver eyes are stern as he nods with his head for me to join them.

"Lennon." Tony beckons him over with a similar nod.

We exchange silver glances before separating, as always, for the needs of our families.

I'm pulled into the center of the group hug, beside Kai, the adults embracing us and each other. Bridie beams, her voice still like a song, "We're together, our family, all of us fae."

"Not me," says Kai. "I'm still human. I don't get it. I thought I was the Spawn. Shouldn't I be super powerful or something?"

"You were the Spawn," says Gerry. "You brought magic

back into the world. Now, you're mortal until your nature chooses your path."

Bridie tightens her grip on her son. "He's one of us, blessed by the fairies."

"Mum, we don't know how much of a blessing this is," I say. "I mean, how are we going to live in the world with silver eyes?"

She tsks. "Glamour. It's the same as Charm. Will your eyes back to human color. You know how. We all do."

I shut my lids and use my Charm, now Glamour, to will my irises to green. A tingle tickles my ocular nerves. When I reopen my eyes, I see that my family has done the same.

I glance over at Lennon. He stands apart from his family, hands in his pockets. Their eyes are back to normal. The adults surround Aaron in the same way my family surrounds Kai. Finding their nature won't be easy for them.

My heart aches for Lennon. Is this his fate, forever the outsider from his family? Then again, that is the fate of all who walk the Wayward Way...

Wait. The spell that dispersed through Kai went out to all descendants of Jade Dragon, Master Stoorworm, and Leannán Sidhe. Are those on the Wayward Way now fae and those on the Glory Road dragons?

Oh. Shite.

Lennon

We return to the *kongsi* and the late shift at the front desk greets us with the usual deference. The head guard, a morose, middle-aged dude named Don, reports nothing unusual happened while we were gone.

Which is weird.

Didn't they feel it, the icy shard of fae or the burning ember of dragon?

Tony, way more interested in his wife and child, rushes upstairs, followed by Auntie Cat, Uncle Roy, and Aaron. I linger behind.

"So, it's all good?" I ask.

Don squints and strains his neck after Tony before turning again to me with a perplexed frown. "Yes, Dragon Son."

"Everyone okay?"

He and his subordinates all nod, but don't look at each other, as if they're hiding something. That's when I sense it. The eldritch seed now burrowed within each of their chests. Each of them feeling it simultaneously, but not revealing it to the others, not wanting to admit to some odd feeling. Except maybe…

"Everyone have dinner?" I ask.

A guard rubs her sternum and laughs. "Yeah. Don ordered from Lee's Garden. I told him they go too heavy on the chili peppers."

The others laugh, too, taunting her for being such a wuss while each rubbing their own chest.

Mass indigestion. That's a good way to explain it. I sure as hell don't know what to tell them.

I recognize the guard who spoke. We went to the same high school before I ran away, but she was a couple of years ahead of me. I once stumbled across her in a nook of the library, sitting on the floor, poetry books scattered around her while she scribbled away in a notebook decorated with unicorns. She'd turned red and apologized, clutching the notebook to her chest. I didn't get what the big deal was. I thought she was doing homework. Now I know. I can sense the silver shard of fae within her.

Those who walk the Wayward Way in the Two Dragon Clan live in silence, suppressing their desire for freedom. Some, like Matthew, follow their path and are banished and shunned. How many are in our clan, already hiding their true nature, who now have something even more powerful compelling them to break free?

I take the stairs instead of the elevator, my steps heavy, though not from weariness. I follow the voices of my family to the living room, going into shadow mode, hiding in the doorway so I can watch without being noticed. Tony sits on the couch next to May, holding her hand. I can sense her dragon ember, but I don't need to, since it's plain from the look of relief on her husband's face. Auntie Cat and Uncle Roy sit on the loveseat, taking turns telling the tale of our encounter with fate. Aaron perches on the ottoman, knees drawn to his chest. Whatever might burn in his chest hasn't yet sparked.

Using Silent Steps, I creep away to my room, close the door, and collapse onto the bed. Alone. Again. I feel like I did that first night I ran away, when I hid on a porch in the Haight, cold, hungry, and afraid. Hollow, cut off from everyone I loved. Is it my fault I'm separated from my family forever? Should I have tried harder to walk the Glory Road? Would I if my parents hadn't died? Leannán Sidhe called me the Flame, as if fate had ordained me to stand in the labyrinth and wear the Yang Pearl. Me, not Dad. How else would I wind up with the Yang Pearl if he didn't die? So many questions. No answers. A harsh breath rattles my chest. Someone must know.

I close my eyes, reach out, and find him settled in an abandoned bird's nest atop Coit Tower.

Hey, dude, I say.

Jade Dragon doesn't reply.

So, am I still your hatchling or nah?

You descended from my human form. Your offspring must also come into their ultimate being, either dragon or fae.

So, if I have kids, they could wind up different from me?

Yes.

That kinda sucks.

He twists in a dragon shrug. *It is what it is. I would have all my descendants be dragons, but the fae take their due. Now you must all seek your true nature.*

How do we do that?

By doing what is in your nature to do.

What if we do it wrong?

Any who threatens the existence of all will be destroyed.

That's not fair. As if he gives a single shit about fair. But he should. He's the one who put us in this position. *How are we supposed to figure this out? Why didn't you tell me from the start what was going on? Why was it all such a big secret?*

The promise of power and the fear of becoming other would have stunted your evolution. Anticipation corrodes growth.

Does that mean we shouldn't tell the others, I mean, like, the other members of our clan, and the Strowlers?

Tell them or not, the choice is yours. Those who fear becoming other will not enter their true nature. As he speaks, he shifts amongst the twigs and feathers before settling with his tail curled around his head.

But...

He heaves a sigh before cutting me off. Looks like dragons get tired, too. I sigh as well, close my eyes, and fall asleep.

The bedroom door opens, but Leannán Sidhe doesn't appear. Tony and Auntie Cat enter and stand over me, staring down at me with their red and gold dragon eyes, no longer hidden by a human filter. My eyes remain closed. Am I dreaming? No. I don't have to see them to feel their presence, their desire for me to remain, to change, to become one of them and be part of their new family.

My nature is what it is. The silver shard in my chest can't be reforged by dragon fire. They know, even if they can't admit it yet. I'm lost to them, have been for years. It's only now they've allowed themselves to mourn that loss.

"He's still my brother," whispers Tony. "Nothing will change that."

"Nothing can," our aunt agrees.

A sob wells up in my chest, but I don't release it. I can't roll over and tell them we don't know what the future will bring as they turn to scale and claw, while silver fills my veins. Can we hold on to what's human within us? Only the centuries will tell.

Auntie Cat pulls the bedding over me, adjusting it around me so I'm tucked in. Then they leave the room, closing the door with a gentle click.

Tears fill my eyes. The sob escapes my lips.

Finally.

Finished.
Because,
if I'm not a dragon,
I can't be
the Dragon Son.

Penny

We sit in the sand on a dune above Ocean Beach, watching the silver waves crash onto the shore. It's a rare, cloudless day, and the sun warms our backs and scorches the tops of our heads, or rather, would scorch if we hadn't already learned a Glamour against its heat. Gerry vibrates beside me, craning his neck every few moments at the least sign of movement.

It's kinda driving me crazy, so I shake his knee. "Da, calm down."

His anxious eyes go merry for a moment. "I don't know why I'm so nervous. The worst of it is over."

The "worst" was carried out by me. We decided Gareth would take it best coming from me, since a straight-up call from Gerry, saying, "Oy, mate, wassup?" would have broken him, and them. That call… I can still see every emotion flitting across Gareth's face as I explained what happened. The only emotion I didn't see was surprise. He knew. He'd told us so. Still, raw feelings filled the room as Gerry took my seat to face the man he loved and nearly lost. Wordless tears flowed. I hugged him for a few moments, dampening his shoulder before letting go and giving them their privacy.

Da takes my hand from his knee, kisses it, and presses it to his cheek before letting go. "Actually, the worst was coming back and seeing you and Kai grown. All those years you needed a father…"

"We still need a father, and now we'll have all three."

He returns my smile before becoming anxious again. "Do you think he'll like it here?"

"Da, he lives in an abandoned train station. Of course, he'll like it here. And it's San Francisco. You can stroll where you please, hand-in-hand, and no one will give you shite."

"But he's never lived in a house before."

"Have you?"

"No." He pauses. "Takes some getting used to. Nice gaff, though."

After Bridie quit her job, we moved into a four-bedroom vacation rental across the street from the beach. Massively expensive, but we have gelt. The contents of Sylvia Lau's jewelry box finally got put to good use. Gerry and Bridie spun their Charm into Glamour, hocking her diamonds and pearls for top dollar while making the fences believe they'd paid a pittance.

The first thought was to return to London, buy a new caravan, and hit the road. Kai was the deciding factor. After all that's happened, our parents don't want to uproot him. Plus, we're not ready to leave San Francisco. We've all changed on a molecular level and we need to figure out what that means.

Gerry's phone pings. He stares at the screen and groans. "Stuck in traffic."

I shrug. "It wouldn't be San Francisco if they weren't."

A lone figure crosses the beach toward us. Gerry shifts into a crouch, ready to spring, his face lit with hope. Then he sees who it is, grumbles, and lays down in the sand, crossing his arms behind his head and closing his eyes.

I want to spring up and run to that figure with open arms, but I stay beside my father, proper-like.

"Hi." Lennon plops beside me, somehow managing to spray sand all over Gerry's face.

Da sputters and glares and acknowledges Lennon's apology with another grumble before shutting his lids again.

"Where's Gareth?" Lennon whispers.

"On his way from SFO," I reply aloud.

"Is it okay if I'm here?"

"Da, is it okay if Lennon is here?"

Gerry doesn't open his eyes as he replies, "Suit yourself, lad."

I roll my eyes. "That's a yes."

We stare at the waves for a few moments, enjoying that sense of each other, close enough to touch, but not. We've spent a lot of time on the beach or in a park amongst the trees, all of us gravitating away from steel, cement, and plastic and toward leaf, grass, and water. I wonder if it's the same for the dragons, but I don't think so. If they're anything like Jade Dragon, then they're drawn to mechanisms and the workings of the world, tolerating the burn of iron for the sake of knowledge.

Speaking of dragons, Lennon didn't show up here randomly. He'd been called to a meeting at the *kongsi* and told me he'd come over afterward. I could ask him about it using Silent Speech, but I don't want to shut out Gerry. I want him to hear how natural things are between me and Lennon, that he's my friend above all else.

"So, how'd it go?" I ask.

Lennon scoops up a handful of sand and watches it slip through his fingers as he replies. "Good, I guess. It was a tele-conference. Me, Tony, Auntie Cat, Uncle Roy, and Second and Fourth Elder. I was formally relieved of my title, which was then bestowed upon Tony. It felt like a board meeting. Anyway, Second and Fourth Elder are now First and Second Elder.

Other Elders will be added as needed, whatever that means. Tony and May are moving to the Chisel Knife compound after the baby is born. Auntie Cat and Uncle Roy will take over the San Francisco *kongsi*."

"What about Aaron?"

"He doesn't want to move or change schools. Tony wasn't happy about that, but they compromised. He'll stay here with Auntie Cat during the school year and at the compound in the summer." He shakes his head. "Poor Auntie Cat. She has to be a mother to another angry orphan."

"She doesn't hate it."

"I guess not. She'll have help this time. She and Uncle Roy are getting married."

I give a happy squeal, although this is hardly news. I mean, who didn't see this coming? "Am I invited to the wedding?"

"Probably. If not, you can be my plus one."

"Cool." I pause, watching the waves roll onto the shore. "It must've been hard for Tony to give up Aaron."

Lennon scoops another handful of sand. "The old Tony never would've done it. Dragon Tony… he was never great with emotion to begin with. Now, he's either micro-focused or looking at the big picture, kinda like Jade Dragon. I always thought they were similar. Anyway, Aaron staying here makes the most sense, so it's done."

"I'm glad, for his sake and for Kai's. This is all so strange. It's good to have a friend to help you figure it out."

"Yeah, it is."

We nudge each other's shoulders as we share a smile.

"Are you okay in the studio by yourself?"

"Better than okay. All I want to do is paint and create. I don't know if it's the fae part of me coming out or just the sense of finally being free."

"Both," says Gerry, his eyes still closed. "I feel the same. I think we all do."

Lennon leans past me to look at him directly. "Um, I told you in a dream, so maybe you don't remember, but I'm sorry my dad shot you."

"I remember. I'm sorry I robbed your da for the sake of Matthew's vile parents. We were all manipulated by that fecker, George, so let's lay the blame at his door and move on."

All three of us exhale. I guess that needed to be said aloud and not in a dream.

Da cracks open an eye. "But if you're courting my girl, you'll do it proper. Understood?"

Lennon's face goes blank. Then he clears his throat. "Yes, sir."

I roll my eyes. "Do I have a say in this?"

"Of course, love," says Da. "You decide what's proper."

Funny how those words make me so happy. I hug my knees to contain my feelings.

"How've I been doing?" Lennon asks me.

I cock my head. "You're lucky I'm a girl who likes mischief."

"I can do better than that," he mutters. He picks up another handful of sand and starts kneading his fingers into his palm. A look of intense concentration comes over his face and his eyes glow silver for several moments before warming to brown again. Then he opens his hand, revealing a large, white opal.

My mouth drops open. "Did you know you could do that?"

Lennon looks as surprised as me. "Not until I started doing it."

I nudge my father. "Look what Lennon did."

Lennon holds out the opal to Gerry, who looks unimpressed. "Remember what Leannán Sidhe said. Each according to their nature."

I grab a handful of sand and start kneading. The granules pour through my fingers. Not in my nature. I wonder what is?

Lennon hands me the opal with a shy smile. "Official courting gift."

"It'll do." I hold it up, admiring the prism of color sparkling in the sunlight. As I do, I notice four figures in the distance crossing the beach toward us. One is striding ahead of the others at an eager pace. I nudge Gerry.

He mutters, "What'd the lad make now? A bloody emerald?"

I nudge again. "Da. He's here."

Gerry springs into a crouch before jumping to his feet, spraying sand all over me and Lennon. Then he freezes, hesitates, terrified.

I reach for his hand and, though I no longer have the Yin Pearl, healing energy flows through me into him. I squeeze before whispering, "Go."

He lets go of fear, doubt, shame, and runs.

Gareth spots him and starts running, too. They meet at the edge of the water, waves crashing and rolling to foam at their feet as they stop and stare at each other, a breath apart. They exchange words. Gareth reaches out, squeezing Gerry's shoulders as if to be sure he's real. Then they fall into each other's embrace, rocking back and forth before their lips meet.

Tears fill my eyes and spill down my cheeks. Of all that's happened–the fear, pain, suffering, and death–this makes it feel the most worthwhile.

Lennon sighs before saying, "That's the most romantic thing I've ever seen."

Those words are a better gift than the opal. I'll treasure both always.

Bridie, Matthew, and Kai watch in the distance, arms around each other, before turning and walking away.

I wipe my cheeks before pressing my hands to my full heart to keep it from bursting. My family. I got them back. I turn to Lennon and see melancholy brush his features. What about him? It's not right. Why couldn't those dragons work their magic for him, too?

I whisper, "I'm sorry your parents didn't come back."

He shrugs. "My dad… he and Uncle George were always going to be the death of each other. Nothing could've stopped that. Mom… I wish she'd left Dad when she found out he was Tony's father, but she loved him and me. I miss her every day, and sometimes, Dad, too."

I wrap my arms around him as his head drops to my shoulder. Leannán Sidhe might've turned a key in our souls, but we're still human. Do fae mourn? Perhaps. We'll find out.

"What next?" His breath is warm on my neck.

Gerry and Gareth stroll down the beach, arms around each other's waists. They pass us and wave. I wave back. They'll be occupied for a while.

I turn to Lennon and feel the silver glint in my eyes. "Let's go to your studio and make mischief."

Next in Series

Learn more about the Dragons of the Crossroads in the exciting prequel novellas. Hidden tells Cat's tale of dark magic, sibling rivalry, and fatal attraction. Dream tells Gerry's tale of forbidden love, murder, and a kidnapping dragon.

To find out more about Dragons of the Crossroads and to purchase more books in the series, please go to loriwriter.com.

Acknowledgments

Heartfelt thanks to my editors: Jennifer Gagliardi and India Cale.

About the Author

Lori Saltis left her heart in San Francisco. She goes to visit it whenever she can afford the bridge toll. She's been an indie author since 2016. She's very passionate about the themes of alienation and found family. Her favorite genre is fantasy because who doesn't want to believe they'll look up in the sky one day and see a dragon?

To find out more about the world of the Crossroads, check out her website loriwriter.com.